INFERNO

FOR INFORMATION CONTACT :
WWW.ARRICKAWRITES.COM

BOOK AND COVER DESIGN BY ARTSCANDARE
BOOK FORMATTING BY DEREK MURPHY @CREATIVINDIE
ISBN: 978-0-578-99583-0

FIRST EDITION: MARCH 2021

10 9 8 7 6 5 4 3 2 1

INFERNO

A Murder. A manhunt.
A desperate quest for the truth.

To my dad, I love you more than life itself,
In this world and the next.

(And to Michael B Jordan, I love you too.)

Prologue

In the beginning, there were several tribes of humans who lived together peacefully. They all prayed to the sun goddess Araya and the moon goddess Luna, deities from another world called Olaria who came to Earth to be worshiped as Queens.

Each month, humans would make a pilgrimage to the goddesses' temple in the heart of the country to meet and celebrate the goddesses and give offerings to them. There were always gifts of food, jewelry, and art. Each tribe brought their best and would try to outdo the next. Some of the smaller tribes who didn't have as much to offer often felt slighted at the displays, and it angered them.

They began to sabotage other tribes' crops and supplies out of jealousy and spite. Once the goddesses found out what was happening, they banished them from the land and advised the other tribes that they were free to leave if any of them felt the same way.

As a thank you to those who stayed and continued to worship, the goddesses bestowed some of their powers upon them. The humans would come one by one to kneel at the goddesses' feet as a gift was provided to them. Some were given the gift of eternal youth, some were given the gift of sight, and some were given the ability to transform into various creatures. Luna herself was able to transform into a great gray wolf.

There were a select few who were very close to the goddesses. They were given the secrets of magic and trained by the goddess Luna to be the gatekeepers of this world. They became known as witches. As with everything in nature, there must be a balance. The ones gifted with eternal youth were named vampires and would require small amounts of blood to keep their youth. Shifters were only able to transform for certain periods of time before they began to lose their humanity and become more like the animals they transformed into. The longer they stayed in their animal form, the harder it was to come back, and they would risk never being able to take their human form again.

The humans who were banished learned of the gifts the goddesses bestowed and became increasingly hateful. Eventually, they began to spread lies and hunt those who were gifted. It got so bad that the witches had to create a veil to separate the humans from them. The only way in or out of the veil is through select witches chosen to be the Guardians of the Veil. The goddesses thought that with the veil in place, there would be peace, but they were wrong. Within the community of shifters, tension grew between the wolves and the others. Luna had taken one of the wolves as her lover and the other shifters felt she was favoring the werewolves.

The wolves did nothing to dissuade them. Instead, they would boast superiority because the goddess had chosen one of them. Luna tried her best to make them all feel equally loved. However, there was still a lot of infighting. One day, the man Luna had taken as her lover was found dead, killed by his own weapon that had been given to him by the goddess herself. Distraught, Luna fled back to Olaria, and not wanting to be without her sister, Araya left shortly after.

Eventually, after years of war, the witches and vampires were able to get all the shifters to agree to a truce. They would split the land and live only amongst their kin. They created a council, and each group would have a representative. The witches were allowed too as they would also speak to some lesser creatures like fairies and pixies who had escaped Olaria when the goddesses first came and chose to stay when they left.

The witches lived in Bordeaux; all the shifters, werewolves included, lived in Alexandria, and the vampires stayed in Lyon. They had hoped with this agreement the goddesses would return. However, centuries passed, and they never again walked Earth. The gifts they had given were passed down through generations, and new powers were created with intermingling. There was peace for a very long time. There even came a time when the werewolves and shifters came together as the Alphas from each tribe were tied together in matrimony. It should have been the beginning of a prosperous time for each group, but it soon became

The Beginning of the End.

Squad Goals

Those were the last words she spoke to me; the last words I'll ever hear from her. My Aunt was murdered, and I had to flee the only home I had ever known. Sitting here on the edge of this building, it's taking everything in me not to jump. I won't die, of course... but after everything I've been through, I just want to feel something other than heartbreak and fear.

Aunt Charlotte and I had a difficult relationship. After my parents died and she took over the throne, she went from being my fun-loving, devil-may-care aunt, to a super-strict Buzzkill Betty. She never wanted to be Queen. She would always say she would rather suffer the bite of a thousand vampires than wear the crown. Funny how things change. I watched every ounce of happiness drain from her eyes when the news broke.

The King and Queen were dead. I was only 9 when it happened, and I didn't understand what was going on at the time, only that my parents were gone, and my aunt now had to take over.

"Yo! What the Hell Sai! Why are you sitting out here alone? We have been looking for you! Have you lost your goddamn mind?" I turn around to respond to the loud and agitated voice coming from behind me.

Storming through the rooftop doors are my two best friends, Maven Taro and Aleksander Marseille. We grew up together in the shifter court. After my parents got married, each of the council members sent an emissary from their respective courts to live amongst the others to learn and broker peace.

Maven Taro comes from the vampire court, the only niece of the reigning Vampire King Charles. She was excruciatingly beautiful, tall and curvy with silky black dreadlocks down to her very ample ass. Her ebony skin was smooth and unmarred despite being a warrior like me. That was one thing I was totally envious of. Vampires never had to worry about a skin care routine. I'm sure even if she didn't work out as hard as she did, she probably wouldn't have gained a pound either. It must be nice being the goddesses' favorite; I would joke with her.

"Relax Mave, she probably just needed to clear her mind." Maven whipped around to glare at Aleksander.

The fury in her eyes only lasted for a moment, though. Once you see Aleksander, and he does his best lady-killer smile, it's hard to stay angry or even remember your name. Aside from his dazzling smile, I can't help but notice he is looking kind of good. Even in the dark, I can see his muscled physique wrapped up in a black, cotton, long-sleeved shirt. His dreads that normally would swing just past his shoulders are neatly stacked on his head in a surprisingly sexy man bun.

Aside from being a tall drink of water, Aleksander is a warlock. He isn't from royalty like Maven and me. He was sent as an emissary despite his status because he was probably the strongest magic wielder in the witch court. It's not surprising though, because his family is directly descended from those who created the veil all those years ago. At eight years old, he was able to cast a memory spell on our teacher so that we could skip school and play in the fields. For five whole months, she really believed we were in class and reported back to our parents. It wasn't until she took a leave of absence and a new teacher arrived that they figured out what we had done. My parents were none too pleased, but Aunt Charlotte couldn't stop laughing. She saved us from being punished severely. Instead of kicking our asses, my parents sent us to bed with no desserts, which was still a big bummer.

After that, Maven came to court and the three of us became pretty much inseparable. There were more emissaries from other courts, but the three of us just had a special connection, which is why I didn't even have to ask them to come with me when I left.

They just showed up, bags packed, ready to go wherever I needed them. It's been like that our whole lives. Whenever we needed each other, we were just there.

"Sorry Mave! I didn't mean to scare you. I just needed to think," I said, partially speaking the truth.

"Think? Really? It looked to me like you were about to jump your sorry ass off the side of this building." I chuckled as I stood up. I don't know why I even bothered to lie. No one knows me better than these two.

"I might have been thinking about it," I say with a shrug. At 5'3", I am the shortest in our trio. I have a naturally muscled physique, thanks to all the running I do both in and out of my werewolf form. Unlike most shifters, I was born with gold eyes that sparkled like precious metal in the sunlight, and when I shifted into a wolf, they intensified even more, as if I needed something else to stand out. My afro is pulled back and held in place by a large scrunchie and the will of the universe. Being on the run doesn't give me much time to style it. Normally, I would have had to get dreads like Mave and Alek at the end of our warrior training, but I was granted an exception as the princess. As royalty, I wasn't even supposed to be in warrior training. I had to beg my Aunt to let me attend, and after several months of secret training with Aleksander, I was able to prove to her that I was capable of being a skilled fighter, and she eventually relented.

In the shifter court, everyone is trained as a warrior. Even in times of peace, we never really let our guard down. Out of all the Goddesses' blessed creatures, the shifters and the vampires were undoubtedly the strongest. Which, of course, made us targets. "Everyone wants a shot at the champs," my dad would say.

I could see the worry flickering in Maven's eyes; it's only been three months since Charlotte's death. We'd been on the run looking for answers to questions we didn't know to ask ever since.

"I'm okay, I promise; I was out here just scouting for the guards. After the last run-in, you know they are going to be on our ass," I reassured them.

"It's crazy that they're even after us; you would think they would be here protecting you and helping us instead of hunting us down," Maven says with a sigh.

"Not to play devil's advocate, but they do believe Sariyah killed the Queen." I shoot Alek a warning glare with just a little too much intensity. Even though he is right, it still angers me to hear it. Being accused of my aunt's murder had to be the worst of all the things I have been through. As if it weren't bad enough to have lost my parents, now I've lost the only other close family I have, and I'm being blamed for it too? If I hadn't known better, I would say the goddesses have a cruel sense of humor.

Not that they didn't have good reason to believe it. Not even six hours before her death, I had pretty much said I would in front of the entire court. In my defense though, she had just torn my lover from me. So yes, I was angry and hurt and confused, and I may have said, "You stupid bitch I'm going to rip your goddamn throat out of your ass," but come on, who is going to take that seriously? Apparently, the council and the court, much to my dismay.

"Down, Sai! He didn't mean it that way." Maven's voice snaps me back to reality and helps me push the awful memory of that day behind me.

"I know," I start to say, when the faint sound of footsteps quiets me.

They came from just below us. "Dammit!" Mave curses under her breath.

I knew it before she even said anything. I could feel the power radiating from them in waves. Even this far up, it was unbelievable.

The Royal Guard is here.

Royal Guardsmen

The Royal Guard is an elite force of warriors hand-picked by the Queens and Kings themselves. Comprised of the top warriors, you have to get an invitation just to be brought to the selection ceremony. While that may seem prestigious, the downside was that you had to give up everything once you were in the Royal Guard.

"How many this time?" Aleksander's voice breaks the uneasy silence between us. Even though his hearing isn't as good as ours, I'm sure the looks on our faces and the way our muscles tensed gave it away.

I can barely breathe as I strain my ears, listening to the heartbeats from down below. I count

15,16...17? Wow, that's almost double. I guess that last ass whooping really set them off. We have encountered the royal guard several times since I had to flee. Each time they came with more and more warriors. Each time, we also sent them back to the capital bruised up with their tails between their legs.

"Is it weird that they've stopped moving?" Maven says, and I close my eyes to listen again and realize Mave is right. I can still hear 17 heartbeats, but they are all converged into one space.

Almost like they're meeting up and waiting on someone.

"Maybe they're playing Rock, Paper, Scissors to see who gets their ass kicked first?" Alek says. After a pause, I burst out laughing and even Maven's eyes show a little humor in them. Even in times of peril, we can always count on Alek to ease the tension.

"Whelp," I say, "let's get this shitshow over with. They've got the same hearing as us, so they know we're here; might as well go greet them. Alek, you'll get off on our floor, make the portal, and grab our stuff. Mave and I will take care of the guards," I say with more conviction than I really feel. Not that I'm worried about having to defeat them. Goddess-given gifts aside, I am pretty badass.

"Y'all are gonna take on 17 Royal Guard members on your own??" he stares at me, brows raised. "Don't get me wrong. I know how seriously badass y'all are, but even these odds are tough? I mean especially since we must go out of our way not to kill them, which is ridiculous if I may say so. They aren't going to kill you!" he says. "They need you to stand trial, but I and Mave are fair game. We had the upper hand last time, but now there are more, and I feel like it would be better if all three of us went together."

"It makes sense Sai," Mave said. "Plus, we don't really have the time to argue. Let's just do this together. In the best-case scenario, we kick ass and get away. Worst case scenario, we die, and you go to prison for some shit you didn't do."

Looking at both of my friends and seeing the determination in their eyes, I could hardly say no. "Alright! Fine, we do this together. As soon as we get to the room, you need to work on the portal! In case they decide to come to us instead of waiting, Mave and I will be ready."

We move swiftly into the building, stopping only to make sure we aren't being followed and to make sure the guards below haven't decided to meet us instead. This nagging feeling that we are missing something just won't go away. As we race down the stairs, my resolve hardens. These aren't just nameless, faceless guards; these are the men and women who have protected me my whole life. Some of them were my classmates. I don't want to hurt them, but I do want to survive. I told Mave and Alek as we were leaving court, under no circumstances would we kill any of the guards. We can kick their ass and knock them out, but they must live! They're just doing their jobs, after all. I'm sure by now, the whole kingdom thinks I'm a traitor. I try to shrug off the wave of sadness that comes when I think about it. To think that anyone would really believe I'm capable of killing my own flesh and blood just sends me spiraling into a depression I absolutely do not have time for.

As we round the corner into the hallway leading to the elevator, I caught Maven's eye. The worry hasn't left but has been replaced with curiosity.

"What's wrong?" I asked her.

She shakes her head, but I give her a look that tells her she needs to spill the beans.

"I was just thinking, all those guards down there, and they still haven't moved an inch. They have to know we're here, and they have to know we are moving...yet they're still in the lobby. That doesn't bother you at all?" A quick listen to the heartbeats lets me know she's speaking the truth. The Royal Guards sent here haven't left the lobby, they haven't moved at all. I'm not sure if they are scared or just looking for an opening, but I damn sure ain't about to find out. "It's just really weird," is all she says with a shrug.

"Let's not look a gift horse in the mouth, Maven. They aren't moving for a reason, but we can use it to our benefit," I say. The ride down the elevator seemed to take forever. We watch in silence as the numbers tick down until we reach floor 12, our floor. In a split second, I feel Maven tense up even more, and before I could even react, she rushes out the door and into the dimly lit hallway.

"Maven, wait!" Alek and I yell at the same time. Our words were wasted as not even a second later, Maven's body came flying down the hall. She slams head-first into the wall beside us and her body drops into a crumpled heap.

Alek and I immediately go on high alert. Maven Taro is by no means a lightweight. At 5'11", she was the tallest woman in our warrior training, and she was in a class on her own. She went toe-to-toe with many of the strongest fighters in court, and she always won. As a matter of fact, the only other person aside from myself who's ever won a match.... the only other person who has ever been able to land more than one hit on her... the only person who could pick her up and toss her like a rag doll with ease... was him.

Behind me, I can sense that Alek has come to the same conclusion. "I'll tend to her, Sai, you go deal with him." I quickly turned to him to gauge his reaction. His face is stone-cold and emotionless. I cannot tell if he feels any of the shock or pain that I do.

"Aww, come on Sai, tell me you're not that scared?" Hearing his voice hits me like a ton of bricks. Memories I don't want to relive come bubbling to the surface; me in his arms under our favorite tree. I force myself to snap out of it. Those memories are nothing but a façade; the man in them left me. He chose the Royal Guard over a life with me, and I'll never forgive him.

Almost as if my thoughts summoned him, I could feel him close in. It was stupid to have turned my back on him; his speed was only matched by his unbelievable strength and charm. He couldn't have killed me, but I could have given him the opening he needed to hurt Maven or Alek if I wasn't careful. It's no wonder he and Alek became best friends. They were two peas in the same devilishly handsome and dangerous pod. At 6'4", he was just an inch taller than Alek and his muscles just as large. Where Alek was most dangerous wielding his magic, he was in a class all on his own. The only son of the head of the fallen werewolf clan, House Gerard. He was undoubtedly lethal.

He is so close I can smell the sandalwood and jasmine cologne he wears. Sweet and earthy, just like him. His breath on my back sends shivers down my spine as my body begins to betray me and my mind starts to wander back to those nights under the stars, nothing but a blanket and the passion between us to keep warm.

Damn it! I need to get him out of my head. It's not like he is here to toss me into one of the king-sized beds and make love to me like our lives depended on it. Nope, he is here to drag my ass back to court and I cannot let that happen.

Only seconds have passed, but it feels like forever. We finally know why the guards didn't bother to move once they arrived. They were waiting for him and once he got there, there was no need for them anyways.

Squaring my shoulders, I finally found the strength to turn around and face him,

With a deep breath, I spun on my heels and looked into the amber eyes I prayed I'd never see again.

"Hello beautiful, fancy meeting you here."

3 Months Prior

"I wish we could lay like this forever, under the setting sun in each other's arms," my eyes flutter open to look at Kai. It's in these moments where I feel the most connected to him. Something feels different about his words today, but as his eyes slowly trace my body and his mouth finds mine, I forget the world. We lay there intertwined, hands caressing each other's bodies, Kai's lips only leaving mine to find the exposed skin of my neck and chest, licking his way down my throat, coming up just to swallow my lips into his. I can feel the pressure rising both physically and metaphorically as he hungrily tastes every inch of me that he can; it's pure ecstasy. He and I are like twin flames, slowly but constantly burning, feeding each other's flames until we are both consumed. We are so lost in our passion we don't even hear the footsteps approaching.

"Gross, will y'all two please get a room?" I lazily roll over to meet the eyes of Maven. Leaning up against a tree, looking as if she would rather be anywhere but here and seeing as she could, this had to be important.

"Technically, as a Princess, all of these rooms are mine. Including secret outdoor ones where I don't wish to be found." Not wanting to leave Kai's arms, I shuffle my body between his legs until I am in a sitting position, still cozying up to his chest but also able to face Maven.

"Why are you here Mave?" Kai demands with an uncharacteristic bite in his voice. Clearly, he didn't want to be interrupted either.

"Hey, no need to be rude, lover boy. Trust me, the last thing I wanted to do was walk in on you two having sex in the garden," she snaps while rolling her eyes. "However, the Queen has demanded your presence and has also asked that I get Sariyah prepared for the banquet."

"What else is there left to do? It's tomorrow for goddesses' sake!" The Queen's Banquet was a large event that happened for every warrior class graduation. It was where the Royal Guard invitations were given and also where each graduate would formally announce their after-graduation plans. This year Queen Charlotte was really going all out; she had witches brought in to hand-curate the floral arrangements. There were so many different types of wine and beer being brought in from all over Alexandria, crafted only by the finest vineyards and breweries. The whole city was bustling with merchants trying to meet with her to get their goods placed on time. Everywhere you turned, there were meat merchants, bakers, ladies selling all types of dresses and shoes, jewelry makers, and painters vying for our attention. It was a complete and total madhouse and by the time everything was selected, I was exhausted and a bit overwhelmed. It was because of all the chaos that Kai and I snuck away. As much as I love parties, I hate planning them, and with Charlotte busy planning her special announcement, Maven and I had been left in charge of the brunt of it. What she didn't know was that Kai and I had an announcement of our own. Kai proposed to me four months ago during one of our sparring matches. I had just given him the most epic of beatdowns. Even Aleksander would have been proud. I turned around, and he was kneeling in full gear, smiling the biggest smile I had ever seen on him. He looked me in my eyes and promised me forever and a day. It wasn't the most romantic setting, but I said yes anyways. He could have asked me in the pits of hell, and I would have said yes. I loved him more than anything in this world and I could not wait for us to be King and Queen together. That same night, we made love right here in this garden, which had inadvertently become our spot.

"You need to be fitted for your dress Sai, and your highness wants me to make sure all your bits are covered this time," she says with a playful smirk. I wore a semi-revealing dress one time, and she just won't let me live it down. How was I supposed to know the seam would rip right above my ass? Kai had whisked me away so quickly I doubt anyone saw.

"Okay fair enough, but what does she want Kai for?" It's not like he had to do any of the cake tastings or oversee the witch to ensure no poisonous flowers were being made. He just gets to show up and look handsome. Maven just shakes her head.

"Who knows," she says, narrowing her eyes slightly, "maybe she is going to be announcing him as her King Consort and wants to coordinate the outfits." Before I could stop him, Kai was on his feet, pulling me up with him. With his hand still wrapped around my waist, he threw what seemed to be a decent-sized rock right by Maven's head. Close enough that I could see a small trickle of blood from the cut as it whizzed by her cheek.

"Screw you Maven," he said with a laugh. "You know damn well I would never do that." Maven stood fully erect now, not willing to shrug off Kai's well-placed throw. Thanks to the healing gifts bestowed by the goddesses, the scratch on her face was already gone.

"It was just a joke Kai," she says, now bouncing on her toes, ready to pounce, "but you could have really messed up my pretty face and I don't appreciate it." Never one to back down from a fight, especially from Maven, Kai moves to meet her stance.

"It was just a tiny little scratch, for you love, I could have done much worse."

"I'd love to see you try; you only got the best of me last time because I was having an off day. But today, lover boy, I'm going to hand you your ass."

"Alright, alright you two, enough of this." I can't help but smile as I step between these two. The love of my life and my best friend, always fighting and picking on each other like siblings, it was quite a sight to see. I turned to Kai and put my hands on his chest. I can feel his heart beating just beneath the surface. Calm and steady, just like him. His muscles bristled beneath my hand as he reached up to grab onto my wrists.

"Go meet with her and then find me back here. We can finish where we left off," I whisper as I lean into him. He bends down to kiss me on my forehead before running towards the gate leading to Charlotte's cottage. At the last moment, he turns around and sticks his tongue out at Maven while making an obscene hand gesture. Maven returns the gesture before turning her focus back on me.

"I don't see how you could be with someone so childish."

"Really, Mave, that is definitely the pot calling the kettle black." We start to head in the opposite direction. On the other side of the compound is Devereaux Manor. This house has been in my family for generations. Every Devereaux child is born and raised here, and eventually, it's gifted to the eldest so that they may bear their children here too. It belonged to my father and then Charlotte, and it was gifted to me on my 16th birthday, and I have lived in it ever since. As we walk the path down to the manor, Maven stops to look at the castle looming in the distance.

"I still don't understand why y'all don't live there," she says. "It seems like a waste of perfectly good space."

"The castle is just so old school; it's only used for important events like this damn banquet and welcoming honored guests. It used to house the royal families and the families of important members of the court, but once the world modernized, it just seemed...extra. Besides, it's just me and Charlotte now, the last of Devereaux line. We don't need that much space anymore." We walk the last few yards in relative silence. Maven no doubts scheming on how to get us into the castle as my mind kept wandering to Kai's weirdness today. It was probably nothing, but I just could not shake the feeling of impending doom. It doesn't take an oracle to see that something sinister is on its way. I just hope that we are strong enough to bear it.

Present Day

"What are you doing here?" I ask him, not willing to break eye contact even though every fiber in my being is screaming to look away, run away, hide. Anything but standing here with this man.

"Well, you know," he drawls, sounding out every syllable in that sexy, annoying way he does. "I heard there was a big-time fugitive around, so I thought I'd pop in and say hello."

"Pop in and say hello?" I scoff. "You didn't seem too interested in saying anything when you decided to join the Royal Guard and leave me. At the anger in my voice, his eyes softened and the smirk he had been wearing slowly dropped. I couldn't help the rage, though. How dare he stand in my face and act like nothing happened, joking around as if mere weeks ago he didn't break my heart in front of the entire court, in front of my Aunt. Pledging his allegiance to her and her crown only, knowing what it meant for us. Once I started, I just couldn't stop. I have never been more hurt or humiliated by one person in my life. This man promised to love me and never leave me, and he lied about both. Propelled by my own fury, I stepped forward and swung. As quick as he was, he couldn't dodge it as my fist landed squarely on his jaw.

"Dammit, Sai, you're not even going to give me a chance to explain?" The blow landed hard enough to snap his head back but even distracted; his reflexes were still on point. In a moment, he was halfway across the room with his hands up as if in defense.

"Hey, come on now, I thought we could be civil about this. After all, it was you who threw me out before letting me explain. And then it was you who ran away from the kingdom, your court, your people, without even a letter." The nerve this man has. That's Kai Gerard for you. Always blunt, even when it's completely unnecessary. I am so angry I can barely hear his words. I rush towards him again, ready to throw another punch, but this time he is prepared.

He dodges it easily and flanks my left side. Just out of reach and forcing me to spin around again.

"Stop running and fight me, you coward!" I screamed at him. This isn't exactly how I imagined meeting him again, but my fury will not be quelled. I needed to hit something. I need to let out all this aggression that has been building since I ran from Alexandria; there is no better punching bag than the man who broke my heart.

"I see being on the run hasn't done anything for your temper," he says, artfully dodging a kick I could have sworn would connect. "I do see your combat skills have gone down dramatically though," I swear I can see laughter in his eyes as he taunts me, knowing just how to get under my skin and push my buttons. At last jest, I can overhear Aleksander stifle a snort.

"Now's really not the time to be laughing at his stupid jokes, Alek," I yell over my shoulder, "how's Maven doing?"

"She is unconscious still, but she will be fine. She is going to be royally pissed when she wakes up," he replies. "Wouldn't want to be Kai," he says a little softer.

Well, there goes that idea; I was hoping she would be able to help me take on Kai to buy Alek some time to get us out of here. It's all on me now. With nothing on my mind but rage and anger, I begin my attack on Kai once more. Sending a flurry of jabs and punches so quickly, he barely had time to duck. Dancing just outside my range, he starts to turn serious.

"You're going to have to be better than that if you want to land a punch Sariyah, you're focusing too much on your emotions, and it's all over your face. I can practically see your next move before you even think about it." He's right but I don't care. All I want to do is distract him long enough to get the hell out of here.

"Why did you come Kai? Was the Council that desperate to have me? Or were they embarrassed that I sent the elite Royal Guard back home limping? What would Charlotte think, knowing that we outsmarted her best and brightest." At the mention of my aunt, his eyes turned deadly cold. Kai was even closer to Queen Charlotte than I was. So close, in fact, she was the only person I have ever heard call him by his given name and walk away unscathed.

His mother and Aunt Charlotte were close friends and after his mother disappeared unexpectedly, she became his maternal figure. It was through her mentoring of him that we met. Goddesses, I hated him at the time. Always so snarky and matter of fact when speaking, he was an absolute nuisance to be around. He and Maven would get into brawls and always had to be pulled apart by the guards. Despite that, he eventually became close with us and the trio quickly became a quartet. Not long after that, I realized I loved him.

"I don't think she would be happy about any of this," he said finally. "This is not what she would have wanted. She would tell you to come home and face what happened."

"She would have wanted to be alive," I hurled back, not caring how much my words may have hurt him. "She wouldn't have wanted to be left bleeding in the throne room as her murderer got away, and her niece was blamed. She would have wanted justice and to be avenged. If you had even given a damn about her, you would be here with me trying to find her killer instead of hunting me down."

He was on me in an instant. Any trace of his earlier playfulness is completely gone. "You know nothing," he growled as he grabbed me by my neck and pinned me to the wall. I could have broken free of his grasp, but his expression had me frozen in shock. His face had become a mask of anger. No, it wasn't anger; it was more than that. It was pure, unadulterated fury. I had seen this look before, but it was never focused on me. The look in his eyes was nothing but hate. I could feel it radiating off him.

"You were the one who shut me out; you were the one who ran away; you don't get to play the victim here. Not with me, Sai. We both loved her, yet you left me there alone to bury her." For a brief moment, I could see the grief wash over him. I wanted to reach out and touch him, hold him, tell him I was sorry and that there wasn't enough time for me to say goodbye. Instead, I gripped his wrist and wrestled his hand from around my throat.

"Now is not the time for this conversation," I said. As much as I wanted to reach out to him, I had to remember that this was the man who was hunting me for a crime I did not commit. It was awful to know that the Council believed I had killed my Aunt, but it was earth-shattering to know that he did too.

"I hate to interrupt what looks like a scintillating conversation, but if you guys are done hate fucking with your eyes, I think it's time for us to go." I had been so absorbed with Kai I didn't even notice Alek had begun to create the portal, let alone finish it and get Mave through it. One glance at Kai and I could tell he didn't either.

"I can't let you go," he said in a low voice. His tone was soft; I couldn't tell if he meant our relationship or me getting through the portal. "Maven and Alek are free to roam as they please. The Council has not put a bounty on them yet, but you need to come home, Sariyah. You need to face the Council and allow them to hear your side."

"My side? I need to allow them to hear my side? They didn't seem too interested in hearing my side when they sent guards to come lock me up. They were going to imprison me, Kai. Throw me in a dungeon until it was time for my execution, and you were going to help them."

"You don't understand Sai, there is so much you need to know; just please don't make this difficult, please just come home. As of right now, they are only looking at you like a runaway princess. If you come back now, it won't be any worse and Alek and Maven won't be hurt either."

"I really wish I could believe you, but I have seen first-hand what the Council does to traitors. It was a part of my royal training, and it is not pretty. I wasn't going to let that happen to me. Especially before I had the chance to find my Aunt's real killer and clear my name." Before he had a chance to react, I kicked his feet out from underneath him and landed a punch to his chest, sending him across the room. I raced to Aleksander's side, going for his outstretched hand moments before sliding into the portal.

Just as I was almost through, Kai was right there at my side. Quick and agile as ever, I could feel his hand reaching towards my waist. He wasn't quick enough though. As the portal slid closed, I dared take another look at him. He seemed to be mouthing something slowly as if he wanted to make sure it was only seen by me. I couldn't be sure, but it looked like he was saying, "I love you."

Alek

"Arrghh," Sariyah said underneath her breath, but Alek heard it.

"You, okay?" he asked.

"Don't worry about me," she replied. "Let's just find someplace for Mave to recover while we lie low," I finished.

He saw so many emotions playing on Sai's face. Hurt, disappointment, anger, and frustration. And she had every reason to feel that way. She had just fought with the one person she had loved the most in the world, the one person she had given herself to. He would feel the same if it were him in her shoes. It was obvious she still loved Kai so much. But she was right; right now, they needed to focus on finding somewhere to lie low while Mave recovered from the heavy blow she had received from Kai. He would talk with her.

The portal he had opened had led them just inside the Toulouse Forest, somewhere near the edge of the Vampire Court. He hadn't had enough time to properly open the portal to lead them anywhere else and with Maven injured, it only made sense to bring her home. It was probably to their advantage since if they didn't know where they were, it'd be hard for the Royal Guards to find them too. They walked over half a mile before coming to a stop at what looked like an abandoned house. Sai went in to check it out just to be sure it was empty. The Royal Guards surprised them this time, and they couldn't take any more chances. While she went in, Alek looked around the house, scoping out any possible exits should things go wrong. When he got back, Sariyah was there.

"It's empty," she said

Alek nodded, and they both went in. Inside was a bit dusty, with a badly leaking roof and pools of water the last storm must have brought. It was a bit messy too, but apart from that, it was okay. It would have to do. Besides, they were only going to be here for a short while, long enough for Mave to recover and for them to figure out their next plan. Sai led Alek to a room void of the wet mess the other rooms had. There were two dusty beds in the room. She quickly dusted one of the beds off and arranged a pillow for Alek to lay Maven on. Alek had carried her on his left shoulder the whole time. He bent down and gently dropped Mave onto the bed, using some sheets to form a makeshift pillow under her head.

Unconscious, she looked so sweet and gentle, he thought. He'd have to remember to tease her about that later. Rising, he winced a little. His left shoulder was sore from carrying Mave. Fit as she was, she was a little heavy. Or perhaps it was the lack of training he had been doing since on the run; it had to be that. Warlocks weren't as physically gifted, but Alek somehow managed to be an exception. He could hold his own against the shifters and vampires in court, and he was always stronger than the average warlock.

"She's going to have to owe me one for this," he said, twirling his left arm in an attempt to get rid of the numbness that had embraced his left shoulder, all the while massaging the shoulder with his right hand for extra relief.

"I'm certain she'd be happy too, Sariyah said, smiling.

"At least someone is smiling," he returned.

"Yeah, grateful for you, who somehow happens to make us laugh even in situations like this," she said.

"Always," he answered. "Listen, Sai; I know you're hurting and all, but..."

"I don't want to talk about it, Alek. Not now," she cut him off.

"When then?" Alek asked. "We've been together since before I can even remember. We have been on the run together, and I can see that there's a lot that's eating you up. So why don't you talk to me?"

She started to speak in an attempt to argue but stopped. He was right. A lot was eating her up, and it'd be pointless to hide that fact from friends. It would also be incredibly unfair to them since they had sacrificed everything to come on this journey.

"You're right. There's been a lot on my mind lately," Sai stated.

"Well, that's why we're all friends, right? We get to share our burdens. You don't have to keep your feelings hidden from us."

"I know. It's just I haven't had enough time to even understand what exactly I'm feeling. It's all so...."

"Overwhelming," he completed.

"Yes, exactly. Aunt Charlotte's death was so sudden. Her last words to me were a warning, asking me to run away to remain alive. I didn't even get to bury her, just like Kai said. Being on the run, I haven't had time to grieve properly and mourn her. Her killer is still out there, and we are no closer to finding out who they are. On top of that, in the only place I ever called home, I was accused of a crime I didn't commit. So there. I'm shocked by her death, overwhelmed with bottled-up grief, angry at her killer, and hurt by all the accusations."

"That's a lot of things to be feeling. It's amazing you've managed to stay this strong." Alek had no idea she had been hurting beneath her smiles all this while.

"Trust me; I'm barely keeping myself together. I feel even worse dragging you and Mave into this mess."

"You didn't drag us. We chose to come, remember?"

"Yeah, and I'll always be thankful. Wouldn't have gotten this far without you guys."

"No need. You'd do the same for either of us."

Sai nodded. "And then there's Kai." She took a deep breath and turned to look at Alek.

"You still love him."

"As much as I'd love to hate him, I still do love him."

"I understand. What you guys had was beautiful."

"Is that supposed to make me feel better? 'Cos it sure doesn't. It only makes me miss him more."

"Yeah, I'm sorry."

"How could he have accepted to come after us? Oh, the balls he has!" she exclaimed.

"You know he was only doing his job, right?"

"The same job that took him away from me," Sai said with so much hurt in her voice.

Of everything she was feeling, the hurt from Kai's betrayal was the worst. The memory of the day Kai joined the elite Royal Guard was still fresh in her head, as ever-present as the pain in her chest.

Sariyah hadn't understood why he had made the decision. Had she done anything to make him angry? Did he not love her anymore? Her mind quickly raced to the moment just before the portal that had brought them here closed. Didn't he say he still loved her? Or was it her mind trying to play tricks on her, making her see something that her heart so desperately wanted to believe? If it wasn't mind tricks, and he did actually said it, why did he make that decision, knowing what it would mean for them? It only made Sariyah more confused and angry.

Who did he think he was, anyway? Leaving her to serve in the Royal Guard and then telling her he still loved her right during a fight, one in which he was supposed to win and bring her back home in chains.

"Oh, the nerve he has!!" she said under her breath.

"I'm sure he had his reasons," Alek said. *He had to have his reasons*, Alek repeated in his head.

"Stop defending him, Alek. He was your best friend, and he left you too, remember?"

"Trust me; I couldn't forget even if I wanted to."

"Then you should be taking my side here and not-"

"I am on your side, Sariyah!" Alek retorted angrily, his eyes piercing into hers. He never called her by her full name. That he did so right now meant one thing to Sai. He was angry. She had hit a nerve.

"I've been on your side since this whole thing began," he continued, softening his tone. "Don't think that I like what Kai did. I hate every bit of it! But like you said, he was my best friend. I know him, and that's why I know that something must have made him make that decision. He loved you, Sai, very much. If you ask me, he still does. You know we wouldn't all have walked out of that fight if he hadn't let it be that way. Look what he did to Mave, He knocked her out and still let us leave with her. Plus, when you attacked, he was completely on the defensive. With how wildly you were throwing punches, he could have easily taken you down or even taken us, hostage, to force you to come with him, but he didn't. Now tell me, why would he do that?"

They were both silent for a few seconds.

"I miss him too, Sai, but there's got to be a reason why he did what he did. There's just has to be," he finished.

She could hear the hurt in his voice as he spoke. He really did miss Kai. But he couldn't possibly imagine how much Sariyah missed him! He wouldn't be able to grasp how deep this betrayal went. He couldn't because he didn't know the whole story about Kai and her. He didn't know that Kai had asked her to be his wife, and she'd accepted. Neither Alek nor Mave knew about it, and it seemed like they would never need to. Kai's decision to join the Royal Guard was almost as good as breaking off the engagement.

She desperately wanted to tell them, but now wasn't the right time. So, she looked up at Alek and said, "I hope you're right. Either way, with or without him, we'd be alright."

Alek feigned a smile and nodded. Then they embraced the silence.

Sariyah

The sun had started to set before Maven finally woke up just as Alek and I had begun to doze off ourselves.

"Goddesses above, what the hell happened?" she groaned quietly. "My head is ringing like a church bell and I feel like I've been hit by a train." Maven slowly tries to rise and take a look at her surroundings. "Yuck, why are we in this dirty room? And why am I on an even dirtier bed? And oh goddesses, what is that smell?"

"It's the mold," I said.

"Sariyah, what the hell happened? I know we are on the run, but this is low even for us."

I couldn't help but to howl with laughter and eventually, Alek even joined in. Leave it to Maven, Vampire Warrior Princess, to be so bougie.

"Ma'am I am so sorry this is not the five-star quality establishment that you are used to. However, I assure you it was the best we could do in the midst of running for our lives," Alek quipped, tears rolling down his face from laughing so hard. Rubbing her temples, Maven began to try and stand up.

"Really guys, what happened. I remember us going up to the room and then...."

I could see the realization hit her. The ever-growing lump in my throat has begun to tighten. I already knew what she was going to say.

"Sariyah, was he really there? Goddesses no, please tell me I slipped and fell or that the Royal Guard warriors jumped me and knocked me out. Please do not tell me I actually got knocked out in one hit by your stupid, arrogant, know-it-all, tattle-telling boyfriend!"

"Ex-boyfriend," I whispered, trying hard not to meet Maven's eyes. Aleksander's laughter quickly died out.

"My apologies. I know how hard it must have been to face him after all this time. Seriously though, how was he able to get the jump on us and how in the hell was he able to knock me out with one hit? He is a good fighter," Maven said a little begrudgingly, "but that's a feat even for him."

"That another issue for another time Maven," I say, "right now, we need to make sure you're okay and ready to travel so we can figure out what the hell is going on."

"Where are we?" she asks.

"The Toulouse Forest, it looks like," I say rather quickly, grateful to talk about anything other than him.

"Yeah, sorry Mave, kind of had to bring you home. Kai being there threw us for a loop and this was the fastest portal I could make and get us through," Alek explained.

Maven's face became as solid and unreadable as a stone statue at the revelation of being in her home again. I never actually managed to get the story out of her about why she became an emissary for the vampires. Her uncle was the current King and, so far, had no heirs. She was the oldest daughter of his younger sister Princess Sarafine, and thus she would have had a direct claim to the throne. Maven's parents died when she was young, so I'm sure that is part of why she came, but she never spoke of home and rarely visited.

I sat and watched her mull over the information, unsure of how she was going to react. After a few minutes, she sighed and just shook her head.

"It's been too long since I've been back; I should probably go see Uncle Charles. Who knows, maybe he might even be able to help us figure out who killed Queen Charlotte."

"You think he would let two fugitives and a possible murderess just waltz into Elysium and just start asking questions?" For the second time today, we both shot Alek a death glare.

"Must you always be so blunt?" I ask, not bothering to hide the bit of anger in my voice.

"While I disagree with his delivery Sai, he does make a good point. If the word has spread that you killed Charlotte, then in the interest of keeping the peace, he would have to at the very least notify the Shifter Court that you were there. Although, with me being his favorite niece and all, I may be able to delay it for a little while."

I'm not going to lie; it sounded like a good plan. Charlotte and Serafine were really close and King Charles doted on his baby sister. If anyone knew about Charlotte's enemies, it very well could be him. Still, I was uneasy; if she couldn't get her uncle to delay notifying the Council of where I was and we weren't able to get away, it could mean I never find out who killed my aunt, but the outcome would be the same if I didn't go at all. I don't think I could face Kai again and win. Not because I wouldn't be able to beat him or at least hold him off long enough to escape, I just don't think I would resist anymore. My heart has taken too much loss and another round with him would be more than I can handle.

"Can I think about it?" I ask, finally feeling both of their eyes glued to the top of my head as I sat at the edge of the makeshift bed, drawing circles on the floor. "We should be safe here for the night and I just need to run and get my thoughts together." And get them off of Kai.

"Yeah, of course, Sai," they both say at the same time.

"I'm going to scrounge around the house and see if I can find some ingredients to make Mave a tonic for her head." Alek turned to the door and left, almost immediately diving into his own thoughts on what he might need. Still feeling her gaze, I finally get the nerve to look Maven in the face for the first time since she woke up.

"Just spit it out already," I say. "But just for the record, I don't want to talk about a certain Royal Ass."

Her face scrunched up as she considered what she wanted to say. After staring into space for what felt like forever, she looked at me and said, "I'm sorry." Then she turned onto her side and closed her eyes. Realizing I wasn't going to get any more out of her, I headed out back. The night was brisk, and the moon was just starting to wane. This was my favorite time to run. I headed deep into the forest, beginning to strip my clothes off to shift as I walked further and further into the brush. I would find them later. Right now, all I wanted was to run until I couldn't breathe and then run some more. Shifting comes as easy as walking these days. The first few times hurt, but after a while, it's just second nature. I can feel the hair growing all over my bare body, thick brown tufts shooting out from beneath my skin, coarse but soft and shiny. The tips of my nails begin to elongate into claws and the bones in my body begin to break and mend over and over as I take on my new form. It takes all of three minutes before I'm standing on all fours, ears perked and surveying my surroundings. The night is beautiful. I can hear the soft scuttling of the woodland creatures hiding beneath the brush, the wind whizzing by as I start to run, heading nowhere and everywhere at the same time, moving too fast to put even the smallest of thoughts together. I haven't run like this in months, and it felt amazing. I could almost forget all of the troubles waiting for me back at the edge of the forest.

Just before sunrise, I shift and start to head back. I can see Alek beckoning for me and I rush to finish getting dressed. I throw on my jacket and jog back to the house. As I shove my hands into my pockets, I am surprised to find an origami flower hidden there. Curious, I begin to open it just as Alek walks up to me.

"Sai, you're not going to believe this!" he exclaims. I shove the flower back into my pocket. There is only one way this could have gotten into my jacket without me realizing and if I'm correct, this isn't something I want to read aloud.

"Alright so talk, what's going on," I demand.

"Sai, you're going to want to sit down for this." Rolling my eyes at Alek, I sit on the bed next to Maven, with one knee propped up on the frame and my elbow resting on it.

"So, what super amazing thing happened?"

"Well, I wouldn't call it super amazing, but it does involve Kai." My stomach lurched. I probably would have vomited if I had eaten anything in the last 12 hours. For the love of the goddesses, why does everything have to lead to him? Bracing myself for the worst, I listen to Alek tell me what had transpired after I left.

"So, I was going through the house finding ingredients for Mave's tonic and thankfully, the forest has a healthy supply of herbs. I made it pretty strong on its own and it should have begun working immediately. However, after about 20 minutes, Maven's head still hurt. At first, I thought that I had messed up somewhere and the tonic wasn't prepared properly, so I made another batch even stronger than the first."

"Even nastier than the first," Maven said from the bed. Alek flipped her a vulgar gesture and kept going.

"Well, once the second one didn't work, I had to really brainstorm. The only thing I could come up with is that Maven's headache didn't come from a physical blow but a magical one!"

"How could that be possible though? Kai doesn't have any magic?"

"That's what we said, but sure enough, I cast a healing spell that negates the effects of magical attacks and sure enough, Maven was back to her normal snarky self."

"So anyways," Maven begins, "once we figured out that it was magic, I tried to remember what happened when I went into the room. I didn't sense Kai at all, and it worried me. I couldn't recall anything. I saw Kai's face for the barest moment and then everything went black. We wanted to make sure there wasn't something I might have seen, but my brain didn't register, so I let Alek take a peek into my mind."

"You did what? When did you even learn to do that?" As gifted a Warlock as Alek was with manipulating memories and thoughts, mind walking was a feat most witches and warlocks had trouble with. It's extremely dangerous and requires precision and focus. If you make even the smallest mistake, you can forever get trapped in someone's memories.

"I was going to tell you Sai, seriously I was. It was a part of a super-secret training Kai had suggested. I had only been practicing for four months before we ran."

I wanted to be upset at him for not telling me, but I know all too well what it feels like to carry the burden of a secret. Instead, I took a calming breath and asked, "Well, what did you see when you went into her mind?"

"I saw Kai, of course, but I also saw a woman with him. She was hovering just behind him with one hand raised, almost like she was holding a shield in place. Which is probably why we didn't see or hear her and Kai until we were already upon them. She had to have dropped the shield in order to blast Maven back. She had long jet-black hair and a dress so tight it could have been a second skin. I mean, you should've seen her. She was curvy and beautiful and had a gorgeous smile. She even winked at me, which at first I thought was weird, but when you think about it, Kai was the one who urged me to learn mind walking, so what if she knew I would be looking?"

"Well, aside from the way-too detailed description of the stunning ebony goddess my ex is apparently running around with... did you see anything else of use?" I can only imagine how pissed my face looked because even Alek's mahogany skin showed a pinch of red.

"My bad Sai, it's just been so long since I saw a pretty woman it took me off guar- Ouch!" he proclaimed as Maven hit him upside his head. She was quicker than I was at that remark.

"Hey now, I didn't mean that you two ladies aren't beautiful."

"Yeah, you're damn right we're beautiful and you best never forget it. Anyways doofus, tell her about the flower."

"Oh yeah, so just before Maven's mind went dark, the lady in red held up her hand and in it was a red and yellow marigold. The red was so vibrant it matched her dress- *smack* -damnit Maven, I'm just trying to be descriptive," he said, rubbing the same spot on his head where Maven had hit him again.

I was already drowning them out. The flower Alek described was sitting right in my pocket. I had figured Kai had probably put it there just as I was going through the portal, but I had hoped it was something personal, something just for me, but clearly, it was a clue to something larger.

"Don't you know what this means Sai?? I was right; there had to be a reason for all this. Now we just have to figure out what exactly it is."

"I think I can help with that." Trembling, I pull the flower out of my pocket. It is still surprisingly uncrushed and still beautiful. Clearly, it's been imbued with some sort of magic to keep it looking so…well…magical.

"Sariyah, where the fu-" Maven's question is cut short as her eyes are drawn back to the flower that was now spinning in my palm. As I spun it, it began to unfold and just as Maven reached out to grab it.

The Marigold began to sing.

Follow me and find the answers that you seek; beware my dears; what you may find, may be sickly and not too sweet.

After repeating the phrase a few more times, the marigold and the sultry voice coming from it went still. The room was dead quiet as we all took a moment to figure out what had just happened. Maven was the first to break from the trance. Hand still suspended in midair she turned to look at me. Her face was a mask of pure confusion; it took her a second to finally speak.

"What the fuck was that and where the hell did you find it."

"It was in my pocket," I started to explain. "I found it when I went to put on my jacket. I didn't get a chance to open it before Alek came to get me about y'all's exploration, so I forgot about it. I thought that Kai had probably hidden it and I don't know; I hoped maybe it was a secret love letter or something." Feeling embarrassed and slightly stupid, I stared at the ground and shuffled my feet. Of course, it wasn't a love letter; how could I have been so foolish. Try as might; I cannot forget that he left me in the most painful and public way. At the same time though, he did risk everything to get us this note.... goddesses, why does he have to be infuriating and so goddamn confusing.

"I get it Sai, no matter what happened, you still love him. I can't say I wouldn't have done the same thing. I'm sure Maven would agree if she could only stop being angry and running men away," Alek said with a half-hearted chuckle.

"This is the craziest shit I've ever witnessed in my life. If it weren't happening to us, I would never have believed it," Maven exclaimed. "So, what does this mean?" she pondered. "Is Kai really helping us or is this some plot to lure us to them so they can ambush and capture Sariyah?"

I had been wondering the same thing myself. It seemed too good to be true. However, it would make sense as to why Kai didn't really fight back. I didn't want to admit it then, but it almost felt like he was conflicted, like he was trying to tell me something without telling me.

"Well, if we had any doubts about going into Vampire Court, they've definitely been squashed now," Maven said, turning around to start gathering our things. "We really have no choice; we have to start finding answers and this is the best we are going to get. Even if Uncle Charles doesn't know anything, he could still possibly point us in the right direction."

Twenty minutes later, we were packed and ready to go. Alek had scavenged some herbs to bring with us along the way and thankfully had found a berry bush growing nearby so we could at least have something in our stomachs. Toulouse Forest stretched several thousand miles, creating a natural barrier around Lyon, the country the vampires claimed. In the heart of it lay the city of Elysium, headquarters to the Vampire Court and Maven's old home. I had never been there before. With all my warrior training and princess training, I didn't have much time to go anywhere. From what I was told, it is as beautiful in the summer as it is in the winter. Both Kai and Alek got to tag along with Maven and Queen Charlotte on some diplomatic visits and I was always insanely jealous. Kai would tell me that once we got married, he would take me all around the world and show me his favorite spots.

Journeying through the forest at top speed, we made it to the other side just as the sun was going down. We could have shaved a few hours off our time if Maven was at full strength, but whatever the Red Lady (that's what we started calling her) hit her with drained her a lot more than we thought.

"Alright, let's stop here to rest," Maven said, coming to a quick stop. Leaning up against a tree, she looked out towards the city that lay just beyond. It was just as beautiful as they described. From our vantage point, I could see the sprawling hills that seemed to go on forever. Lush bushes of flowers grew in so many colors that it looked like an artist just threw paint in the air and flowers sprouted where it landed. I could see what looked like orchards of fruit trees. The castle was majestic. I could see why Maven thought it was weird that we didn't use ours. The towering castle stood at the border of the estate. Its stone walls are pristine and impenetrable. It loomed over the city like an invincible protector. The houses around the castles were just as grand. Looking more like mini-mansions and lavish estates. I wouldn't say it put the Shifter Court to shame, but I could definitely see how going from living here to there would be an adjustment.

I could only imagine what was going through her head. When I look at the city all I can see is wonder and amazement. I'm sure when she looks at it, she is reminded of the pain of losing her parents and whatever pushed her to come to Alexandria. After resting for a short while, we decided to head into the city. Maven took the lead as these were her old stomping grounds.

"I brought us around the back so that we didn't have to cut through any cities and answer any unnecessary questions. After all, we still don't know if the word has spread about Queen Charlotte and we can't risk the Royal Guard being alerted," she said from the path ahead of us. "We don't really know what we're walking into, so it's better to come from the back in case we have to make a quick exit." We were a hundred feet away from the back gate to one of the gardens when I noticed the air starting to shimmer. I had been around Alek long enough to spot a portal opening when I saw one.

"Guys we have trouble," I yelled out. Whirling around, Maven and Alek spotted the portal just as a figure appeared out of it.

"No need to be frightened," the figure said, the voice soft and feminine. Now fully out of the portal, the woman speaking stood before us. She had to be in her late 40s with brownish-red hair down her back. Her brown eyes were like deep pools of chocolate and they twinkled as she smiled at us. "I am a friend of the King. He sent me here to greet you and bring you to him at once."

"Well fuck, we made it all the way here just for him to already know we're coming; why couldn't he just send the portal to the forest so we didn't have to walk? Would have saved us a lot of time," Aleksander said incredulously.

"Seriously Alek? That's what you're worried about? Not the fact that my Uncle, who is definitely not psychic, knew we were coming and prepared a woman who is clearly a witch to come greet us?"

"Oh yeah, that too, I guess," he retorted with a sheepish grin. "I'm just saying though it would have helped."

"Your Uncle is thrilled to have you come visit Maven; we mustn't keep him waiting. Besides, I'm sure the sooner you can leave, the better." At that, she darted her eyes towards me.

Shit, they know...they absolutely know, I thought.

"Well, shall we?" she said. Her outstretched hand beckoned to the gate we were about to go through.

"Let's get this over with," Maven said, striding forward. "By the way, witch lady, what is your name and how do you know my Uncle?"

"My name is Josephine, and as I stated, I am a longtime friend of King Charles. He helped my family many years ago and I have made myself of service to him ever since." Smiling and lost in whatever thoughts she had about her and King Charles, Josephine led us through the garden and into the castle through what had to be a servants' entrance. "Normally, we would have greeted you in the main hall, but we understand discretion is necessary." Once again, her eyes locked onto mine. I held her stare this time, mentally daring her to try something. I would rip this castle apart before I let anyone take me hostage. She gave me a smile and wink and turned her attention back to Maven and the hallway we were going down.

At the end of the hall, there was a large ornate door. Some of the symbols were recognizable, the sun, the moon, and possibly a set of fangs. It was as ominous as it was beautiful. As we approached, the door began to creak open. The room beyond was lit with a soft yellow glow, and the scent of fresh coffee and muffins wafted to us as my stomach let out a very loud, noticeable growl.

"Ah yes, the servants managed to bring nourishments up just in time. Feel free to help yourselves to anything you would like; however, I would highly recommend the strawberry muffins. They are absolutely heavenly."

Once we were inside the room, the door behind us slammed shut. I could probably rip it off if I had to, but I hope I won't need to. Across the room, behind a large mahogany desk, sat a burly man with sad eyes. His black hair was braided neatly back and situated underneath a jeweled crown. As soon as he saw Maven, his eyes lit up. Even though she tried to hide it, I could tell Maven was happy as well.

"It's been too long Mavey." His thunderous voice filled the room. It was deep and rich like molasses put into words. "I've missed you so much. It's sad it took this long for you to come visit."

"I'm sorry...I was just, you know...busy...doing stuff." Maven's gaze did not meet her uncle's. Instead, she looked everywhere but in his direction.

"So, you finally finished your study, I see, very kingly. Although seeing you in here with that gaudy crown on kind of takes away from its presence." Maven began to pace the study, caressing the books and artifacts that line the walls, trying desperately not to look as excited as she was. The King's eyes never left her. It was as if it was just him and his niece in this room together, the rest of us as unimportant as the books on the shelves.

"I see your lying hasn't gotten any better over these last few years. Although your wit seems to have grown," he boomed. "What exactly have those shifters been teaching you? Is sarcasm part of their warrior curriculum?"

Maven turned around to look her uncle in the face finally, "There's nothing they could teach me about sarcasm that I didn't already know. After all, I had the best teacher," she said with a wicked smile. "Anyways Uncle, unfortunately, as much as I have missed you, this isn't a social visit."

As if he finally remembered we were in the room, King Charles finally looked at Alek and me. "Yes, I see," he mused. "You brought the witch and the Devereaux child with you."

"Child?" I proclaimed. "I'm much more than a child. I am the heir apparent to the Shifter and Werewolf Court; you should show me more respect."

"Sariyah," Maven scolded, "that's my uncle you're talking to, lest you forget he is King, we are in *his* court and we need *his* help."

"It's okay Mavey; she is absolutely correct. But tell me heir apparent, how much respect should I show the young woman who is currently being accused of murdering the Queen Regent of her very same court?"

Shit, I thought as my blood ran cold. With all this back and forth between Maven and her Uncle, I had momentarily forgotten why we were here in the first palace.

"I am sorry, Your Majesty; I didn't mean to snap. I assure you though, the rumor of me killing my aunt is false, I'm being framed, and we are actually here trying to prove it. If you could please forgive my lapse of decorum."

"No need to apologize, Princess," he said, enunciating my title. "I am aware of you being framed and it is because of that I did not immediately notify the Royal Guard. And even though, as we speak, they are attempting to gain entrance onto my land; I am keeping them at bay long enough to provide you with the answers you're looking for.

Let us begin with the Order of the Marigolds."

"Josephine dear, you better take over from here; after all, it is your order." King Charles beckoned his lady friend to his side. Alek, who had been silent this whole time, was now a flurry of questions.

"What is the order of the Marigolds? Who is a part of it? Why was it founded and what does it have to do with the Queen's death?" He was rattling off questions faster than we could count.

"Slow down son, and let the lady talk," King Charles said, his deep voice now full of complete seriousness, promptly cutting Alek's inquisition short.

"All your questions will be answered dear, I promise," Josephine crooned. "So, you already know I am a witch, but I am actually a little more than that. I am an Oracle and one of the seven Guardians of the Veil. I have other talents as well, but those are the most important. What do you know about Oracles and the Guardians of the Veil?"

"My mother is one of the Guardians," Alek states proudly. "The Guardians are seven of the strongest witches who were descended from the first witches, given the knowledge of magic from the Goddess Araya. They watch over the gates between the realms. No one can go in or out of them without their permission."

"Very good! You are absolutely correct. The only thing you are missing is that each guardian does not know who the others are. It was a safety precaution should any of us become compromised. And now what about Oracles?"

It was my turn to speak.

"Um I know that Oracles are witches who can receive prophecies from the goddesses. They are usually pretty gifted in other forms of mind magic and are the only ones with permission to do some of the forbidden spells like mind walking and skin walking."

"Exactly right Sariyah, mind walking, which allows you to walk through someone's mind and memories, and skin walking, which is being able to put your consciousness in someone's mind and see what they see in real-time, are some of the most dangerous spells to cast. If not done right, they can leave you trapped in someone else's subconscious.

"Goddess above," Mave grumbled, "that's creepy as hell." She darts her eyes to Josephine. "Is that how you knew where we were? Did you mind walk into one of us?"

My skin suddenly began to crawl. The thought of someone being in my mind without me ever realizing it gave me the heebiejeebies. I looked at both Mave and Alek to see if they felt the same uneasiness I did. Their faces confirmed they did.

"Oh, my goddesses' no!" Josephine said with a hearty laugh. "I foresaw that you were coming weeks ago, so I knew where I had to be and when." Even with her laughing it out, I still couldn't shake the thought of her possibly being in my head. I made a mental note to figure out a way to block someone from being able to get into my head if I make it out of this alive anyways.

"Ok, so what does all that have to do with this Order of Marigolds?" I asked once my mind settled, and I felt, sure enough, she wasn't in there.

"Long ago, before any of you were born, I was here with Charles playing in the fields when a prophecy came to me. It spoke of children born under a reaping moon gifted with extra powers from the goddesses. They were said to be the most powerful generation to come, a new beginning for our world as one of them would be a goddess reincarnate. Eyes yellow and red, this child would be able to walk amongst the goddesses and wield their power. These children would be in danger as there was a force at play. A force that would not want to be overshadowed by these children."

The room was completely silent as we digested the information. How could such a prophecy be hidden? Who are these kids? Have they even been born yet? I had so many questions, but before I could figure out which one to ask first, Josephine continued.

"The prophecy was so strong it left me in a weakened state. My body and mind were not used to receiving something so powerful. You see, over the centuries, the goddesses have sent fewer and fewer prophecies. As the world modernized, there was just no use for them and thus, they did not bless many with the sight as often. I only know of two others, and they've never seen more than a mere glimpse of trivial things to come. I told the council, but they would not take me seriously. I had even enlisted my good friend Charles here to get me an audience with his father, the King, but no one would listen. They had lost faith in the Oracles' power, and I was just a child then. They thought I was just making it up.

"Alas, over the next few years, no child was born more special than any other and the prophecy and the crazy Oracles were forgotten."

"I never forgot you though," King Charles said softly. As he looked at Josephine, you could tell there was more than friendship between them.

"That's right," she quipped. You always made sure to check in on me after your father sent me away. Didn't want me filling his son's head up with silly nonsense, he said. I went back to my home and prepared for what I knew was inevitable. It took 15 more years, but sure enough. During the winter solstice, the moon rose, but this time it was burning red. It looked like it had been engulfed in flames. I knew then what it was, and I came to warn Charles.

"The next day, it rose and set like normal; I thought maybe it was a fluke. But sure enough, a few weeks later, it happened again. It kept happening every few weeks until, at last, the year ended. By that time, Sofia and Kalen had been married, and Charles was made king."

My throat tightened at the mention of my parents. I couldn't hide the hurt on my face, but I willed every tear away from my eyes.

"I am sorry Princess; I know how young you were when you lost your parents." I could see the sincerity in her eyes. However, when I look at King Charles, I see a flicker of what looks like rage. When I blinked, it was gone.

"Did you know them?" I asked

"I did; I knew them as well as your Aunt. I had met them a few times when they came on diplomatic engagements between shifters, vampires, and witches. I knew your father as well, Aleksander, such a strong man; it is no wonder he was able to marry one of the Guardians, although quite the ladies' man. I knew it would take quite a woman to get him to settle down."

"Alright, enough of the walk down memory lane," Maven interrupted. "What happened to the kids born under the freaky moon."

"At first, nothing, no one displayed any remarkable talents and, once again, my prophecy was dismissed. However, seven years later, kids born under those moons started to disappear; only to be found dead. The Order of Marigolds was created to find out who was killing these kids and stop them.

"Your Aunt Charlotte was a part of the Marigolds; she was actually the one who named us."

"Who could have done something like this?? What kind of monsters kidnap and murder children and why?" I couldn't believe what I was hearing. I can only imagine the burden Charlotte had to carry all of these years, no wonder she didn't want to have a position of power. She had a front-row seat to how it corrupts.

"A selfish person, the kind of person who only thinks of themselves and their own greed. Someone who would do anything not to be seen as weak and to have their power removed from them." King Charles' words were full of venom as if talking about this very person made him ready to kill. The rage I thought I had seen earlier was back in his eyes and there was no hiding it.

"The kind of person who would kill babies for being a threat is the same person who took my sister away from me," he turned his glare and practically spat the words out. As if the taste was poisonous to him as well.

Kalen Devereaux

Is Anyone Not a Liar?

"No." I shook my head and glanced at each of them in turn, Aleksander, Maven, Josephine, waiting for them to tell me I had heard wrong. Of course, I did. "Ha!" My lips even stretched into a strange grin, hysterical laughter threatening to erupt at any moment.

I blinked as memories skipped through my brain, proving the king wrong. When I was seven years old, I went through a phase of not being able to sleep, convinced that monsters were hiding beneath my bed and in the closet. Every night, my father went down on his hands and knees, made a great show of sliding his hands across the floor under the bed, and pulled out a candy wrapped in cellophane which he handed to me with a flourish. "Nothing but sweetness for my sweetheart," he said. And what about the bedtime stories, the games, the surprise gifts he made me promise not to show my mother?

"No," I repeated. "There must be some mistake."

King Charles watched me, the hard edges of his words replaced by a gentle half-smile. "There was an investigation, child. It took place over many months, so many people were afraid to speak up, afraid of what would happen to them if ..."

I knew what he was going to say, and anger flared inside me. "No! Don't you dare say it!"

I picked up the object that was closest to me, a golden vase with crimson flowers painted around the base, and I threw it on the floor. I didn't care that it was smashed into a hundred pieces. I didn't care that a shard had cut my foot, a bobble of blood forming on my skin. I didn't even care that it might have been priceless.

Breathing too fast, I narrowed my eyes at King Charles. "I don't believe you." My voice was low, little more than a growl.

"Sariyah, I'm so sorry." The king reached out as if to touch me but slowly dropped his hand. The look on my face said it all. I didn't want him anywhere near me spreading his lies.

"It wasn't him." I paced the room, barely seeing where I was going. "It must have been someone else, someone who looked like my father. These people are lying – I know they are. Ask them. Speak to them again, and they'll tell you they got it wrong."

Maven reached out a hand, and the gesture was too much for me to bear. I sank to the floor as the room began to spin. Nausea welled in my throat and I clamped a hand to my mouth but breathing through my nose was too difficult. Strange choking sounds filled the room, and it was several moments before I realized they were coming from me. Tears stung behind my eyes and spilled down my cheeks. I buried my face in my arms and waited for it all to go away.

"Sai." Someone took my hand in theirs, and I felt an arm wrap around my shoulder as Maven's hair created a veil around us. "Sai, please," she said.

I raised my head enough to glance at her, and I could see in her eyes that it was true, "My father would never ..." I began.

Maven didn't speak. She pressed her cheek against mine and held me close, and that was when I knew it was true. I closed my eyes and waited for the darkness to swallow me whole. If I never opened them again, I wouldn't have to deal with this... this pain. The room spun out of control, and instead of fighting it, I fell...

Maven

Is she dead? Goddesses, I hope she isn't dead. As soon as King Charles said Sai's dad's name, Sariyah began to spin out. Maven didn't think she would have ever expected her dad to be the villain in any story. Let alone a story about a power-hungry psychopath who kills children.

Mave knew better though. She saw him in her house the day her parents died: he and one of his cronies. Maven's mom had seemed really agitated that they had come so late and wanted her to go to the maids' quarters. She pretended to leave, but as soon as the coast was clear, Maven hid in the closet by the door. She didn't see it happen, but she heard it. Maven heard her mother's voice scream out in pain and heard her body fall to the floor. And then laughter. His laughter. She would never forget the way he sounded as he murdered her parents. Then they walked right out the front door like nothing had ever happened. Maven had never told her uncle what she saw. But from that moment, she vowed to kill him, with her bare hands, if necessary. Unfortunately for Maven, he was killed in battle a short while later. There was no news of his crony. Since she couldn't get the big bad wolf, pun intended, she would have to settle for the lacky instead.

"How long is she going to be like this?" Mave asked, looking around the room. Aleksander looked like he wanted to throw up, Uncle Charles looked like he would destroy a small village, and Josephine just looked sad.

"Too long," Uncle Charles said finally. "This is not the way I wanted to tell her. I'm sorry Maven. After all this poor girl had been through, the stress of this was too much. She will wake up, I'm sure of it, but not until she has processed all of this and regain the mental strength to carry this burden. It could take hours; it could take days. There is really no way to tell."

Looking at Sariyah, Maven had to hold the tears at bay. Sai has lost so much already; Maven doesn't know if she will even want to come back. She knows she wouldn't.

"What should we do now? Mave, the king, can only hold the Royal Guard back for so long before they might just outright attack."

"I don't think the shifters have a commander that stupid," King Charles said with a snort. "Attacking my domain is a declaration of war and I highly doubt anyone wants that. They will wait until I tell them it's ok. My warriors are loyal to the crown first and everything else after; they will not yield."

"We can't let them have Sariyah," Maven exclaimed. When she wakes up, she is going to want to know more, and she can't find out anything from a cell, or worse, from the after world.

This couldn't have happened at a worse time! Dammit Sai, I thought I was supposed to be the drama queen. She wanted to throttle her again but knew it would be no use. Sai won't wake up until she is ready. And Maven very well couldn't blame her if she didn't.

"Alek, do you think you could make us a portal out of here? Maybe back to the house in the woods? I'm sure we could make base for the night."

"That isn't going to work. For one, I am a hundred percent certain that they would have combed those woods by now. They would definitely be lying in wait if you returned. Also, your witch cannot create a portal here. It has been spelled so that only those who I give my permission can use magic here."

"Well, can't you just give him permission?" Maven asked. "Goddess, what's with all of the theatrics today?

"If it were just that easy Mavey, I wouldn't have brought it up."

"Maven, Uncle Charles, please call me Maven." It's not that she particularly hated the nickname. It's just that the only people who had ever called her that, aside from Uncle Charles, were gone.

"We can't let them have her," she said again. She looked at both Alek and Uncle Charles, hoping one of them have an answer.

"I'll be able to help," Josephine says from behind her uncle. She was so quiet Maven had forgotten she was there.

"Help us how?" she asked.

"Well, I already have permission to use magic, so I can create a portal for you; I can also make sure it leads to a hideout that even the council knows nothing about, much less the Royal Guard."

"That would be extremely helpful," Aleksander says as he stands; he had been doing some healing magic on Sariyah, it looks like. "We can go as soon as you are ready. And um...do you mind if we take some of these snacks?" he said, eyeing the table hungrily.

"Yes, of course," Josephine laughed. "It should only take me a few minutes, and then I'll have you on your way."

They stood back as Josephine worked her magic. It was beautiful to watch. A witch of her level didn't even have to recite the spells anymore. She could just weave the signs and the magic worked itself. Even Aleksander hadn't mastered that yet. Her movements were so fluid and precise, it was like watching a dancer on stage. The only person more in awe was Uncle Charles. You could tell by the way he watched her move and the light in his eyes that he really loved her. Maven had to make a mental note to ask him about it later. For most of what she could remember, he had been alone. He withdrew deeply into himself after Maven's mother had died and only the council and key members of the guard were even able to see him. It was one of the reasons Maven didn't like visiting. As much as she knows he missed her and loved to see her, she was also aware of how much she looked like her mom and how much it hurt him even if he would never say it out loud.

"Alright, you guys can walk on through now; I can't tell you where you specifically will be landing just on the off chance you were ever interrogated but know that you will be safe for as long as you need. And Aleksander, you'll be able to make a portal out as well." Josephine stepped aside so they could walk through the shimmering veil of the portal she had created. Maven loaded up as many of the snacks and water she could carry and Alek picked up Sariyah, cradling her in his arms much like a baby.

"Mavey- I mean Maven," Uncle Charles called out, correcting himself. "Please stay safe. And, umm, come visit more often. You know this place could use more of a woman's touch."

"I will definitely be around to visit once we get everything cleared up. I think you have the woman's touch already covered though," she said with a wink and a nod toward Josephine.

Mave followed Aleksander through the portal before she could hear either of their responses.

Maven

It was three days before Sariyah woke up. Neither Alek nor Mave wanted to leave her alone. They slept in shifts, each keeping watch over her. They couldn't be sure what state she would come back to. All that information had to have taken quite a toll on her to cause her to shut down so hard.

For the first day, Sai really didn't say anything; she opened her eyes and got up to go to the bathroom, but whenever Alek or Mave would ask her anything she'd just stare blankly at them. As if she could hear but not see them.

The safe house the portal led them to was a large three-bedroom, two-bathroom compound completely surrounded by a lush green forest. During the day, when she wasn't sitting in one of the rooms staring out the windows, Sai would wander around the house. And at night, they'd hear her leave to shift in the forest. It went on like that for another week.

It was 5 a.m. and Sariyah Devereaux wasn't back from her run yet. Alek and Mave had breakfast started in hopes that she might eat something today.

"I think she is really broken Alek. I thought when everything happened with Kai and Queen Charlotte, she definitely broke, but this has her completely gone, and I don't think she will come back. And why would she? The only good thing she had left were memories of her parents and now those have been taken from her too. What are we going to do if she stays like this?"

"You could be right Mave, but I also just think she needs time, and as long as we're safe here, she should have it. I don't disagree that she's broken, but I think she can be put back together. She just needs to know we are here for her. We can't push her too hard. Once she's ready, she'll talk to us. In the meantime, let her run, let her wander, let her find a way to come to terms with everything that has happened. When she needs us, we can just be there for her."

"I don't know how much more I can take of this Alek. She's like a freaking zombie," Mave said, mostly joking.

"Then leave. If this is too much for you, please go."

Shit. Shit shit shit. This is not the way I wanted her to start speaking again.

"Sariyah, I am so sorry I didn't mean it like that." Before Mave could even fully turn around to face her, she was gone, back out the door, running to goddess knows where.

All because I couldn't keep my stupid mouth shut.

Sariyah

I wish I could say I felt bad for leaving like that. I wish I could say I felt anything. I don't anymore. Not since that final bomb was dropped on me. Everyone in my life has lied to me: my parents, my aunt, my ex-fiancé. Maven and Alek haven't yet. Although avoiding any conversations with them for the last week was surely starting to drive them away.

I know I should talk to them, but I feel like I'm about to vomit every time I try. My palms get sweaty, my heart races, and I feel like I'm dying. Besides, what am I supposed to say? "Hey guys, I know we just all found out that my dead parents were actually psychopathic murderers, but let's all go get ice cream! Let's not forget that my dad killed Maven's mom!"?

She probably hates me. How could she not? At least, now I know why she ran from Vampire Court. She was probably searching for answers like I am now. Now that we have them, where do we stand?

"Hey, Sai, please don't run again; we just want to talk," Aleksander huffed. I heard them following me a few miles back. I thought they had given up. Even when I'm in my human form, my speed is unbelievable; Maven no doubt would have caught up with ease, but Alek definitely had to work a little harder.

"If I wanted to run, you'd know it," I said. Not with any malice, just matter-of-factly. "If you're here to tell me you're leaving, you don't need to bother. I completely understand. I'll be fine out here."

"Wow....Just like that, the High and Mighty Sariyah Devereaux dismisses us. Come on Alek, let's leave the princess to her royal duties."

Maven's words hit me like hot daggers being thrown straight from the kiln. I knew she hated me. I just didn't think she would show it like this. Not one to back down from a fight and damn sure not about to let her see how much her words hurt, I spun around, ready to smack the shit out of her just to start a fight.,

"Hey now, hey now," Aleksander said, stepping between us. "I love a cat fight as much as the next person, but I don't think this is the time for it."

"How dare you Maven. How dare you act like that to me? After everything we have been through."

"Exactly Sai, everything WE have been through. I know that you're dealing with a lot and you have every right to be upset. Especially after the stupid comment I made this morning, but you have no right to just dismiss us like we're common peasants! We are your friends! We risked a lot to be with you, not because you asked us to and not because we felt like we had to. We did it because we love you even when you're being a total asshole."

I laughed. I laughed hard. Not because what she said was funny, but because I truly didn't know what else to do. Maven looked so serious and so angry I just couldn't help it. I laughed until my eyes were watering, and my friends looked at me like I had finally lost my mind.

"Uh, Sai? You good?" Alek's look of concern becoming more defined by the second did nothing to stop the laughter from engulfing me. Pretty soon, I had to sit down to keep from falling.

"We should totally just push her into the bushes," Maven said over her shoulder to Alek. Looking down on me, some of her earlier anger vanished. "I mean, seriously we could probably get away with it." Half smiling, half looking at me like I was having a psychotic break, she moved into a stance as if she would actually do it.

"Girl," I growled, finally able to choke back the laughter. "If you try, we're both going down and I know how much you'll hate pulling sticks and bugs out of your precious locks." I crouched on all fours as I spoke, ready to evade or attack depending on her next move.

"Ladies, ladies, let's not do this, okay? Maven, Sai is finally speaking. Maybe we should count that as a win?" Alek inched closer to us, still trying to keep us apart. "And Sai, I completely forgive you for being kind of prissy. Let's just all get along and try to find the real bad guys huh?"

After a tense second Maven and I, both loosened our stances. "Look Sai, I know you're mad at us and also overwhelmed, but we aren't leaving you. Not now, not ever. You'll just have to get over it," Mave said with a shrug.

"I'm not mad at you guys; I've been avoiding you because I figured you would be mad at me. I mean, my dad killed your mom and my Aunt covered for him." I start to shift back and forth feeling really uneasy and not quite able to meet Maven's eyes, afraid of what I might find there.

"Why the hell would I blame you for that? You were a child. You can't take responsibility for the actions of your parents. And it's pretty shitty that you think I would even blame you. What kind of friend would that make me?"

Before I could answer, her arms were around me, pulling me into a tight but comforting hug. I was finally able to release the tension that had built up inside me and for the first time in a while, I cried. And not a pretty cry. It was the ugly, snotty, puffy-eyes, sore-throat cry. I don't know how long we stood there like that, but Maven never let go. She held me until I couldn't cry anymore.

Aleksander left and had come back with warmed-up breakfast and coffee. The smell of bacon and biscuits definitely lifted my spirits. I had been so depressed and mopey I'd hardly eaten save for the few woodland creatures that had the misfortune of crossing my path while in my wolf form.

I scarfed everything down in a matter of minutes. I really underestimated how hungry I was. Maven sat next to me drinking what smelled like coffee with animal blood (nice to see I'm not the only one eating forest creatures), and Alek had a blueberry muffin he was silently picking apart.

"So, what's next?" I asked. "I still need to find out who killed Charlotte. Finding out my dad was probably the reason she died gives us something to work with. Whomever was working with him before he died, probably who killed her. I think we should work on finding out everything we can about who my dad hung out with." I look at both of them, trying to gauge what their response would be.

"Let's go to the witches' realm," Aleksander said thoughtfully. "I think I might know someone who can help. Worst-case scenario, we would get free drinks."

"So, we're going to a bar?" I asked. "With me on the run for murder...we are going to go to a bar?"

"Not just any bar. The Witches' Brew. It's filled with all kinds of degenerates, none of whom would be too keen on the Royal Guard popping up. We should be relatively safe long enough to get the answers we need. Besides, even though it's in the witch realm, it's nowhere near Court."

"You had me at free drinks," Maven said with a laugh. "What about you Sai? Or is the Princess too classy to slum it in a bar."

I picked off a piece of my biscuit and threw it at her, laughing as she caught it in her mouth. "Of course, I'm down, so long as I get to wear something sexy. Who knows, if the Royal Guard does show up, I want Kai to eat his heart out."

We packed up our makeshift picnic and headed back to the compound. "We leave at 8 p.m." Alex shouted over his shoulder as he rushed to the apothecary in the back, no doubt, to stock up on any supplies we may need.

"Be ready and we might even have time to stop for your slutty dress," he said with a wink before disappearing.

Maven and I shared a look before each disappearing to get our belongings. It felt nice doing something normal, even if the circumstances were completely abnormal. I really hoped we could find answers soon. The sooner I was able to clear my name, the sooner I would be able to start uncovering the next mystery: Who the hell were King Kalen and Queen Sofia Devereaux?

The Drinking Game

"Sariyah Devereaux, you've really outdone yourself this time," Alek crooned. "If you weren't my friend, I'd definitely try and shoot my shot."

The look he gave me was anything but friendly. We had managed to snag some new clothes from a local shop. Alek and Maven went inside while I hid around the back. They brought me a few to select from and I had chosen the least-revealing but still very hot v-neck crop top with a short, tight-fitting skirt. Both of which were in a gorgeous shade of lapis lazuli. The outfit hugged every curve, and my chest was all but spilling out. I looked more like a harlot than a princess, but that was the goal.

Maven decided to go with distressed jeans – in black, of course – I thought, rolling my eyes. She paired it with her normal boots and long sleeve shirt, thankfully in a flattering shade of lavender. Alek, ever the ladies' man opted for a button-up t-shirt that he has chosen not to button all the way. His muscled chest peeked out just enough to give any lady lucky enough to be near him a good eyeful. He also wore jeans and black boots.

The three of us sauntered into the bar that was definitely located in a seedy part of town. Outside there were several gruff-looking men smoking cigarettes and staring us down. Aleksander's imposing presence was probably the only thing keeping them from pouncing on Maven and me the minute we walked past.

"When you said this place was full of degenerates, you weren't exaggerating," I said, taking in our surroundings. For what it's worth, the place was pretty clean. There were two bar areas, one on the first level smack in the middle of the lounge with an assortment of sofas and tables surrounding it. There was a small space that I'm guessing was supposed to be a dance floor, but there was no one on it. The second bar was on the top level overlooking the floor. The lights up there was a little dimmer, creating a more sinister atmosphere.

We walked up to the main bar and took seats. "A whiskey and coke for me and whatever the ladies want," Aleksander said, flashing his smile to the beautiful bartender.

"Anything for you, handsome," she slyly replied.

"I'd like vodka on the rocks straight with a bag to vomit in," Maven chimed in. The latter part is a dig at Alek's over-the-top flirting

"I'll have a whiskey neat." Both Maven and Alek turned to stare at me like I grew an extra head. I am not an avid drinker like they are. Not because I don't like to drink, but because I usually end up shoeless and stumbling around. But Kai was always there to protect me.

"What?" I exclaimed. "If we're rolling with the big dogs tonight, we might as well go hard."

They shared a glance before shrugging their shoulders at me. "It's your funeral Sai," Maven stated with a laugh. "Although I wouldn't go too hard, my little lightweight, I think Alek is going to be too preoccupied to carry you home." She nodded her head in his direction.

I turned to look at the situation unfolding. Alek had slid a few seats away toward the end of the bar and was currently whispering something in the bartender's ear that made her giggle and blush.

"Goddess, leave it to him to find romance on a mission," I said back to Maven.

"That boy would find romance in the pits of hell if he could." He must have heard us talking about him as he pulled away from the bartender's ear long enough to give us a wink and a smile.

"Not to be rude," I said a little loudly, "but do you think we could get our drinks?" The bartender perked right up, this time fully blushed, not realizing she had been neglecting her job to flirt with my friend.

"I'm sorry ladies, your drinks will be right up." I look back at Alek, who is now currently giving me a playful scowl and an obscene gesture.

Stick to the mission, I mouthed.

I am, he mouthed back.

I had no idea how trying to bed the bartender would assist us, but I digress. The pretty bartender brought us our drinks. As she was about to turn away, she must have gotten the courage to ask whatever she wanted to ask because she darted her eyes to Alek, who was in a deep conversation with another patron and asked us.

"Is he really single? I know he's your friend and you have no obligation to answer, but I just don't understand how someone so good-looking could not have a girlfriend."

"It's because he's really dumb," Mave answered.

I swatted her arm. "Maven don't be rude." I turned back to the bartender. "What's your name, sweetie?"

"My name is Annabella, but everyone just calls me Bella."

"Okay Bella, yes he is very much single. He is very kind and has an amazing soul. If you are looking for a charming man who will move realms to please you, he is definitely the one. However, just know, we are all warriors and if you decide to go down this path and hurt our friend, we will stop at nothing to hunt you down."

Her eyes widened for a moment in pure fear, but I could see that she was up for the challenge. She didn't back down and instead gave me a fierce smile. "I wish I had friends as protective as y'all. But I assure you I would never intentionally hurt anyone." At that, she walked away to continue whatever scintillating conversation she was having with Alek.

"Damn Sai, how are you going to tell me not to be rude and then go all psycho protective on the poor girl."

"You remember the last person he tried to date," I said hesitantly, "I don't want to see him hurt like that again. I meant every word I said to her."

Thirty minutes or so had passed when a man came and tapped Alek on the shoulder. He pointed up to the second-level bar and mouthed something I couldn't quite read. I didn't have to wonder for long as Alek stood up and motioned for us to follow. We walked past a very pouty Bella and made our way up the stairs.

As we made it to the top of the stairs, we couldn't hear the music any longer, even though we couldn't be more than a hundred feet away.

There must have been a spell cast to keep unwanted noise from floating up here or floating down.

Sitting in front of us, sprawled across the massive couch to the far right of the bar, were five witches. Two males and three females. One was definitely a couple, as they were currently intertwined in a way that would make the goddesses blush.

As we approached them, the two untangled themselves enough to greet us.

"Hey, cousin," the female said. She had fiery red curls spanning the length of her back; she had to be at least three inches taller than me, although it was hard to tell in her current position.

"Sariyah Devereaux, Maven, this is my cousin Jezlyn. Jezlyn, these are my best friends."

"It's so nice to finally meet you." She stood up to give us hugs (much to her male friend's disappointment). "Alek has told me so much about you guys it's like we're already friends."

"Yeah, we heard one of you killed a Queen." The statement came from the other male in the room. He looked to be as tall as Aleksander and just as handsome. He had dark hair and dark, broody eyes. As if he had something terrible on his mind.

"Wow Remy, I told you not to mention that," Jezlyn said sternly. "Besides, Alek says she's being framed, and he wouldn't lie, so play nice."

"I am so sorry," she says, and she really does look it. "Remy doesn't have a filter sometimes, but I promise he means well and won't say anything."

"It's fine; pretty soon, the whole world will know unless I can find the proof I need." My eyes haven't left the sulky Remy. I know Jezlyn trusts him not to say anything, but I still have an air of uneasiness about how he so readily accused me.

"So aside from Remy, these are the rest of my friends. Amethyst I've known since we were infants; our moms were best friends. She pointed to the petite blonde sitting on the far side of the couch. Her blue eyes surveyed the three of us, but she did not say a word.

"That brown-haired girl behind the bar is Ellie, she works here, but we also went to school together!"

"Hey, it's nice to meet y'all!" she said, smiling. "I already got your drinks from Bella, so I'll have them right over."

"And last but not least, this tall drink of water is my boyfriend, Armel." Armel stood at least six feet tall, if not taller. He had jet black hair cut low but still had some curls. His brown eyes flittered to us as if to say hello, but they landed back on Jezlyn. She returned to his lap and stared at us expectantly.

"So, cousin, we are here like you asked. How can we help?"

Family Secrets

"Well, it's like Sariyah said," he began. "She is being framed for her aunt's murder. We are trying to figure out the clues as to who did it. I thought you might have something in your possession that would be able to help us. A scry? I think it's called."

"That's a pretty big ask dear cousin," Jezlyn said musing over the thought. "How about we play a game and if you win, I'll tell you whether or not you're right."

"What's a scry," I whispered to Maven. She looked as clueless as I did. Aleksander looked at us, waiting to confirm whether we wanted to play.

"What the hell? It can't be worse than anything else that has happened," I say, taking a seat in one of the empty spots.

"I'm game," said Maven, who sat cautiously close to Remy. She noticed me looking and blushed a little, but she blushed, even more, when she noticed Remy also looking at her. The look in his eyes showed her was sinfully delighted to have Maven so close,

"Alright guys," Jezlyn stated, taking a drink from Ellie, who had just come around the counter.

"Let's play the drinking game."

***

The drinking game was the adult version of "Never Have I Ever." Instead of using our fingers, we instead had ten shots each. We all took turns stating something we had never done in hopes that the others had and would need to take a shot. The person with shots left at the end was the winner.

It started off innocently enough; there was never have I ever cheated on a test, never have I ever stolen something from a shop, etc., but after a while of no one taking a shot, it began to get more vulgar. Thanks to Alek, and not surprisingly, Remy.

"Never have I ever gave someone I just met a lap dance," he said using his most sultry voice and eyeing Mave.

"I'm sorry you wasted your turn with that one, but I have never done that," she said, laughing nervously. In all the years I have known Maven I have never seen her like this. Not that she hasn't dated, but she is a certified maneater. I have literally seen her bring men to their knees, yet she is acting like a schoolgirl around Remy.

"Well love, there's no time like the present," he said, leaning close and wiggling his eyebrows. He was so close I thought he was going to kiss her. Maven just sat there frozen. Afraid that he would kiss her or afraid that she might like it, I'm not sure.

"Ah-hem, I think it's Maven's turn since no one took a shot." Maven turned her head to give me a grateful smile, relived to be semi-off the spot.

"Actually, had you two not been swooning over Remy, you would have noticed someone did take the shot."

Aleksander brought my attention back to the group. So far, a few of us had taken some shots, but it had been mostly a standstill. As I looked around, I was surprised to see that the person whose shots were one short was none other than Amethyst.

The shock must have been clear on my face because she and the others started to laugh.

"Don't look so surprised, Sariyah Devereaux," she said in a quiet voice. "I may look like a doll, but I've got a little spice in me."

This was the first time she had spoken to me directly. Her voice was silky sweet and perfectly matched her looks. I would have never imagined she would do something so scandalous, but looks are very much deceiving.

"No one is innocent here," she said, looking around at all her friends. They all nodded their heads in agreement.

"Anyways, it looks like we might just lose," Armel said, pointing to all the empty glasses in front of him. Both he and Jezlyn were out already mostly due to the sex stuff. Alek, Remy, and Ellie are all on their last shot and Maven, Amethyst, and I each had four.

"It's my turn, but I'm pretty wasted and can't think," Amethyst said, "someone else take my turn."

"Why does it matter if someone takes your turn?" Remy asked, "you still might have to drink."

"Touché, but I'd rather still pass," she said drowsily.

"It's ok I'll go," I said, "besides, I have a pretty good one. Never have I ever committed murder."

I thought it would be funny, considering the circumstances. I did not actually expect anyone to take a shot. As I looked around, waiting for the laughter I was sure to erupt, it never came. Instead, after a few quick glances, Remy, Jezlyn, Amethyst, and Armel all took a shot.

"Well....umm... okay then," Maven started. "So are we going to just bypass this or..."

After a few moments of super awkward silence, "There really isn't much to say. A bad guy did a terrible thing and we stopped it." Remy's eyes went dark as he reflected back on whatever happened.

"Well.... that's enough of that," Alek said nervously. "We all have our secrets, and we aren't here to judge, but it looks like we won, cousin. So tell me, do you have the scry?"

"On that note I'm going to head out," Remy said standing. "I no longer have any interest." He nodded to Armel, who also had gotten up to leave.

"We shall leave you ladies and Alek to it." As they walked toward the back of the room, Armel turned back to shout to Maven, "If you ever find yourself back in this neck of the woods and you want to take Remy up on that dance, I'm sure he wouldn't mind."

Remy's dark eyes lit up for a moment as he looked back at Maven and winked. Then he playfully pushed his friend through the door, and we were left with witches.

"Okay so now that the fun and games are over, can we get the scryer cousin?" Alek asked again, a little more impatiently this time.

"It's not so much an object as it is a person. And you can ask her yourself if you want her help."

We all looked at her confusingly. "Well, how do we find this person? I wish you would have told us that to start with. We are being hunted down by Sariyah's ex and the Royal Guard; we really don't have time to kill."

"Cousin, let us not forget you came to us for help. We did not have to take this meeting. Besides, the scry is already here and you've been drinking with her."

"You're the scry?" I said, bewildered.

"No," she said with a laugh. "I do have some talents, but that one, in particular, belongs to Amethyst."

"Hmmm...what's mine?" Amethyst said, still feeling the effects of the alcohol. *At least I'm not the only lightweight here*, I thought to myself.

"Ellie," Jezlyn called, "do you mind making her a tonic? She is going to be of no use to us in this condition."

"Already ahead of you," she said, walking up with a steaming mug. "I prepped this as soon as they said they were looking for a scryer. She is such a lightweight I'm surprised she isn't worse off."

"Lightweight schmite weight," Amethyst mumbled as her friends sat her up to drink her brew. Within a few minutes, her eyes were clear and her words more coherent. I had to remember to get that recipe before we left.

"Of course, I'll help. I was skeptical when you first came in, not going to lie. The people who usually come looking for my powers usually have nefarious reasons. But if it's to clear Sariyah Devereaux's name, I'll do what I can."

"Wait, so you knew what we wanted from the beginning," I said with a chuckle. "Then what was with the theatrics."

"I had to make sure you were trustworthy. Anyone who can make Remy say more than a few words is definitely someone I could trust."

"Well, I guess we should thank Mave for not running this one-off," Alek said with a wink. If Maven weren't across the couch, I'm sure she would have smacked him.

"Alright, so I already have my ball," from under the couch, she pulled out a large crystal ball nestled in a sparking silver stand with filigree designs swirling around each of its three legs. "So how this works is we will both place our hands on the ball. I will infuse it with my magic, and the ball with function as a bridge and a mirror."

"Oh, so this is almost like mind walking?" Maven asked curiously.

"It's similar yes, sisters but not twins. Where Mind Walking takes the witch directly into your consciousness, scrying sends out the energy into the fabric of time and space and creates a vision. It's also a lot safer as there is no risk of getting stuck within someone's mind, but that's why details are important. The better you can see it in your mind's eye, or the more specific your request is, the clearer the ball's picture will be. It's not as precise as mind walking and sometimes the visions can be distorted or misinterpreted."

"Be clear and stay focused, got it," Maven said. "Alright, let us get started. I am going to be the one who does this. I need to go back to the night Kalen Devereaux killed my mom and get an image of what his crony looks like." *Sorry Sai*, she mouthed, noticing me wince at the mention of my father.

"As the crystal is a transfer of energy, I will be able to see what you see and then I can draw it on paper once we are done."

Amethyst and Maven sat on the floor, hands touching the ball for over an hour. Every now and then, Amethyst would mumble something to Maven about focusing her mind and Maven would grumble back.

It was interesting to watch. From the moment they touched the crystal ball, a smoke-like substance began swirling. It would constantly change color and shape over and over. Watching it felt like I was the one in the trance.

"I got it," Amethyst said finally. "Bring me the paper," she yelled out to her friends. "Quickly, don't lose focus Maven, we are almost there."

As soon as Ellie handed her the paper, she began scribbling furiously. She didn't open her eyes until it was done. Maven rested up against the side of the couch, looking exhausted but satisfied. *Coolest shit ever*, she mouthed at me, too tired to vocalize.

Ellie and Jezlyn both looked over Amethyst's shoulder as she drew. "Alright, finished," she exclaimed. When Jezlyn got a better look at the drawing, her face went pale.

"Oh my god. Are you sure this is him?" She looked positively sick.

"Yeah, of course I am," Amethyst said back, "why, do you know who this is?" She gave Jezlyn a puzzled look, clearly concerned with her friend's reaction.

Maven wiggled over and looked at the image. "Yes, that's him, exactly how I remember him. You did an amazing job."

"Hey, don't hog the image," Alek said, and Amethyst handed him the canvas.

"Alek no, don't-" Jezlyn yelled, trying to grab the canvas out of his hand. It was too late. He had already seen it.

"How in the hell," he whispered. "It can't be." He started at the picture with the same fear and recognition that Jezlyn had.

"Who is it guys? It's clear that you know him," I asked softly. Clearly, it was someone to whom they were close.

Without looking away from the figure drawn on the canvas, he spoke, his tone so low and full of pain I almost couldn't hear him.

"It's my dad."

Truth Sucks

"Well, fuck." I wasn't really sure what else to say. As I was still dealing with finding out that my parents were psychopaths, I hadn't the slightest clue how to comfort Alek.

"Wait, so your dad assisted Sariyah's dad in killing my mom." The room was deadly quiet. The goddesses must have a cruel sense of humor. How else could you explain the fact that we all were best friends whose lives were intertwined so deeply and terribly?

"Maven I am so sorry," Alek started, but he was hushed by Maven's hand.

"Don't," she said, still clearly reeling from this revelation. "It's not your fault any more than it was Sai's. You can't help who your parents are."

How Maven could remain so calm and so impartial, I did not know. If I was in her position, I would have probably gone scorched earth.

"Umm can we go back to the safe house now," she asked meekly, refusing to meet either of our eyes.

"Yeah, I'll umm, make us a portal," Alek said, trying to put some distance between them.

"I'll help you cousin, that way, it will go a lot quicker." Jezlyn rushed to her cousin's side and whispered something to him. Whatever it was must have given him some small comfort as he stood a little straighter and began to get to work.

Jezlyn was right about it going quicker. They were able to create the portal in about half the amount of time and in the meantime Ellie, Amethyst, and I made small talk and exchanged information so that we could hang out again once this was over. Maven sat in the corner quietly; her face didn't relay any of the emotions she had to be feeling. Once the portal was up, we exchanged hugs and stepped through.

Standing in the living room of the compound, everything felt so surreal. We got answers that we needed, but they only led to more questions and more damaged hearts. Maven quickly whisked away to her room and left Alek and I standing there without a word to either of us.

"Well, I guess we're the shitty parents club," he joked morbidly. "I'm going to go try and wrap my head around this. Call for me if you need me." His room was in the same wing as Maven's, and as he neared her door, he looked as if he was going to knock but then changed his mind went to his room.

I was too restless to go into my room, so instead I went outside to run through the woods. It didn't take long for me to get consumed in the wilderness and push today's problems off to tomorrow.

I didn't stay out too long this time. I came back around 2 a.m. and Maven was waiting for me. I could sense her worry and agitation before she spoke.

"He's gone," she said. "Alek left us a note." She shoved it into my hands then stormed away

I have to find out what happened, and I have to do it alone. I love you guys and I am sorry. I'll stop by Vampire Court and tell Josephine to get you if I'm unable to return. I love you and I'm sorry.

"Damnit Alek. I hope you know what you're doing," I whispered to no one.

I get why he thought he needed to do it alone, but I had so many questions too. It wasn't fair to just leave us behind, but I'll have to yell at him later. For now, I'll just say a silent prayer to the goddesses for his safety and wait for him to come back.

He was only gone for two days, but it felt like weeks had passed. Maven and I were eating a dinner of rabbit stew and some vegetables that Alek had made grow in the garden out back when we heard footsteps coming from the foyer. Maven whipped around the table so quickly her spoon fell after she was already gone. By the time I got there a few seconds later, the portal was shimmering closed, and Maven was interrogating Alek like a prisoner of war.

"Well, what happened? What did he say? Did you kill him?" She was firing her questions off too fast for them to be answered.

"No Mave, I did not kill my father. Not that I didn't want to, I just wasn't able to see him in person."

"Well, I didn't really expect for you to do it, just kind of hope. But did you get any answers at all?" She slowed down just enough for Alek to sigh a response.

"Yes and no. I'll explain it all; I just need to sit down."

We moved into the living room and waited for him to begin.

"Well, I went home, but he wasn't there. My mom said he was out helping a friend, so I decided to wait. When my mom let him know I was home, suddenly, his trip needed to be extended another few days. We talked over the phone.

"He knew what I was calling about. Apparently Jezlyn had the same idea I did about confronting our parents. She went and asked her parents, and they informed my dad."

I held my breath as he continued.

"He told me that he and Kalen were good friends, and when Kalen became King and took his role on the throne, my dad became his advisor. They had known about the prophecy and didn't believe it at first. But then suddenly, kids started exhibiting strange amounts of power they couldn't wield themselves and wound up hurting other people. They felt that the prophecy must have been misinterpreted and that the kids would be the danger instead of being in danger, so Kalen, my father, Sariyah's mom, and a few others decided to round up the kids and take them to a safe place so that they could be trained to use their powers. There was an accident and many of them died."

"But that doesn't explain why they killed my mom?" Maven said angrily.

"I know I'm getting there Maven." Alek said quietly.

"Apparently, another group wanted to use the kids as weapons, and they began hiding them. Your mom was one of them and when they confronted her, she attacked them and she was killed.

"That's the story he gave me. That's the web of lies he told to try and get me to understand how he could possibly have sided with a murderer and child killer."

"So, you don't believe him then," she said.

"Of course not; he couldn't even face me to tell me the lie because he knew I would be able to read right through him. My father has always been a terrible liar. That's not it though, he wants me to join him. The so-called mission he was on was to find the other members of the group and finish what Kalen and Sofia started."

"Like hell, you will," I said sternly.

"Really Sai, of course, I would never join that merry band of psychopaths. But it was so scary hearing him talk about it. I can tell he really does believe he is doing the right thing. I did ask him about the reaping moon. I thought that if we could narrow down the year it happened, we might be able to find whichever kids were left before they do."

"Well, what year was it?" I asked, not really wanting to know the answer.

"1998," he said, confirming my suspicions. Exactly 23 years ago; the year we were born.

It couldn't have been a coincidence that Alek and I were abnormally strong, even for those blessed with abilities from the goddess. But once we found out his dad helped my dad, it all started to click into place.

"Shit," Maven gasped, "that was the year you guys were born right." She had the same realization that I did. "But why didn't they kill you too?" she asked, more to herself than anybody else.

"It makes sense, but it also doesn't make sense," I said, thinking out loud. "And to make matters worse, the only people who could answer that are dead."

"Well... about that. In order to get me to come to his side, he gave me a piece of information in good faith. He said your parents are alive Sai. That Charlotte couldn't bear to kill her brother and instead imprisoned them somewhere underground."

Excuse me, What?

"My parents are alive? What do you mean my parents are alive?"

I stared at Aleksander, demanding a response. If it wasn't one thing, it was another. How many more things will the goddesses send to break me? The parents I mourned. The parents I missed. They'd been alive this whole time, hidden away and guarded by my aunt.

"How do we know he isn't lying Alek; how do we know this isn't just some trick to lure us into a trap." I couldn't wrap my head around this. The familiar darkness started to surround me, but I push it away instead of falling victim to it this time. Instead of focusing on my shock, hurt, confusion, and sadness, I focused on the two emotions burning like flames in my soul. I focused on the betrayal, and I focused on the anger. The pure unadulterated anger. I had been lied to by everyone I was close to—my parents, my aunt, and also Kai. With him being the one who gave us the clue that led us here in the first place, there is no way he didn't know. That betrayal hurt the most.

"I know it sounds crazy Sai, but I believe it's true. However, the only people who knew where they were imprisoned were Queen Charlotte and the witch who performed the spell, which if I had to guess, was the woman who was with Kai." What Alek was saying made sense. After all this time, I had completely forgotten about the mystery woman in red. She seemed to be the only one who could provide the answers we needed but short of asking Kai, we had no way to reach her.

"Aleksander, do you think you could reach out to Josephine and see if she can make a trip here? She was the closest living person to my aunt aside from Kai; maybe she might have some more answers for us."

Alek sent word to Josephine, and she arrived two hours later, stepping through the portal that formed in the main hall. She looked as beautiful as ever. Her hair was pulled up into a neat bun and she had a stern look on her face.

"I'm assuming by the urgency of the summoning you must know."

"That my parents are alive or that Alek's dad helped kill Princess Sarafine?" I asked bitterly.

If she felt any trace of my anger, she didn't show it. Calmly she took a seat across from us.

"I wanted to tell you; I just couldn't. After everything went down, a witch appeared to each of us. She cast some sort of spell that forced us to keep quiet to anyone who didn't already know. It was another one of Charlotte's safeguards. As well as the final location of your parents."

"It's easy to blame a dead woman. She isn't able to defend herself or her actions, so why not just put everything on her instead of taking responsibility for your own actions that led us to be here?"

"Sai, that's not fair and you know it," Maven whispered. "You know your anger is misplaced. It's not Josephine's fault Charlotte isn't here to incur your wrath, and you don't get to berate her in her place."

Maven was right, but I didn't even have the energy to say anything. Instead, I shrugged my shoulders and looked at the furnace above Josephine's head.

"So, do you have any idea where she could've trapped them?" Aleksander said.

"No, we don't. We have tried looking ever since we found out she had died. On the off chance that her death freed whatever spell was binding them, we couldn't allow them to roam free."

"We tried to ask Kai, but he refused. He said that things were in motion beyond our understanding and that you, Sariyah Devereaux, would be the key. I think that was his way of helping without going against his duties as a Royal Guard Captain." Josephine looked at me as if this latest revelation from Kai was going to suddenly give me the answers.

"I have no goddamn clue what he is talking about." I don't bother to mince words. "Trust me if I had any inkling that my parents were alive, I would have scoured the earth to find them. I am just as in the dark as anyone."

"This is exhausting," Maven said, slumping even further into the couch. "The more answers we get, the more questions we have, and it doesn't seem to be going anywhere. The only constant is shitty parents and murder."

"Heavy on the shitty parents," Alek said in agreement.

"Maybe we should just go back," I said. "We have a lot of information and even if we don't know exactly who killed Aunt Charlotte, we do have enough to show that it wasn't me right?" I look around the room at them. "Do you think the council will listen?"

"I mean, on one hand, if we were able to get them to listen to us, there is enough reasonable doubt to plead your innocence. On the other hand, though, finding out your aunt has been lying to you about your parents could also be seen as a motive. Goddess willing, they even listen to us. They might just lock you up regardless." Alek made some very valid points.

"I hadn't thought about that. Okay, so what about the Order of Marigolds? Can't you testify to what you know?" I looked back to Josephine.

"Well, now that everything will be out in the open, it may be enough of a loophole for the spell keeping us quiet."

"Will it be enough though?" I ask.

"We are forgetting one important part," Maven said. "How do we even know we can trust the

Council? From what we have learned, Kalen went around pretty much unchecked. Who's to say other members weren't in on it as well?"

The room fell silent. There was a certain uneasiness about what Maven stated. It should have been obvious, but it never crossed my mind that there could have been even more people involved in my father's plot.

Maven went on, "If we go back to Court, we might as well go to the dungeon in your dad's garden ourselves. Although hopefully, they would put us in the main prison. It's much nicer than that musty old place." The latter part, she said, musing to herself.

"What are you talking about?" I asked her. I had been through all of the gardens on our property, and I had never seen any names let alone my father's name.

"We only have one prison and there are no gardens bearing my father's name. I would have seen it."

"It's not an official name, I guess. But I definitely overheard two of the servants calling it that. They were bringing something to the Queen down there. I assumed she had a special prisoner or something and never really thought anything about it."

"There is no goddamn way my parents have been living in a garden at Court this whole time," I said, almost laughing. "That would be too crazy even for us. You must have misheard them."

"No, she is probably right. Charlotte probably wanted to keep them close in case anything happened. I wonder. That would have been incredibly clever, hiding them where no one would even think to look," Josephine stared into the distance, deep in thought.

"So, I guess it's settled. We are going to go look for a hidden dungeon in a garden I still don't believe exists in the kingdom where I am surely to be captured. As soon as I set foot in Alexandria, the Royal Guard is going to know."

"Well," Alek states, "I guess we will have to hope for the best."

Finding Devereaux

"I can't believe we are actually doing this," I mutter to the empty room. After running away to find my aunt's killer, I am heading right back to the place it happened. Right back to the council. Back to Kai.

I don't care what they say. There isn't enough luck in the world to keep me safe once I go back. Damn it, it's why I left in the first place. Everything in me is telling me not to go. Whoever killed Charlotte is out there looking for me too. She used her dying breath to warn me to get away, and yet I'm running back into the fire.

I couldn't convince them otherwise. Alek, Maven, and Josephine had their minds made up. My parents being alive took precedent over clearing my name. I mean, seriously, how much help could two people who have been locked away for 14 years be?

I am trying to wrap my head around everything that has happened these last few months and I just can't. Whenever I try, I feel that familiar darkness wrap around my consciousness, threatening to pull me back into that deep sleep. I almost want to go. Anything would be better than walking into this hot ass mess of a family reunion. What would I even say to them? Hell, what would they say to me? Would they be sorry? Or would they attempt to finish what they started?

I have so many questions. I throw myself back onto the bed in the room I currently occupy and lose myself in my thoughts. This could be my last day of freedom. It could be my last day alive if the Council has their way.

I hear the sound of footsteps coming down the hall; they fall silent just outside my door. There were some hushed whispers followed by a knock. I ignored it all. I'm not ready to leave. Maven could stand outside my door for the rest of forever and I don't think I'd ever be ready.

"I know you know I'm here Sai," her voice barely above a whisper, but I can still hear it perfectly. "I know this is hard; I know you probably have mixed feelings about seeing your parents, but what if they have the answers we need?"

"Why is no one asking the most obvious question," I say in a normal tone. "Why is no one asking, 'what if they are behind it?' what happens when we get there and they look me in my eyes and they tell me that this was all a part of some sinister plan to get free and finish what they started? Which includes killing me and Alek, and who knows who else."

I sat up as I heard the door open, but Maven stays at the threshold. "I can't imagine what you're going through Sai and I'm not going to pretend like I can. You've been dealt blow after blow. However, more than your feelings are at stake here. If your parents are behind it, worst case scenario, they are already locked up and I'm sure the council will have creative ways to make them pay. But if they aren't behind it, they could help us find out who is and why. After that, you can deal with whatever unresolved feelings you have."

I was about to respond when I heard commotion from the living room. Maven and I both sprang into action and raced down the hall. The sounds came from the kitchen. When we ran in, Alek was standing in front of a broken glass pile, which I'm assuming made the noise.

"What happened?" I ask. I saw it then—Kai's marigold. I had left it with my stuff when we first arrived, so I'm not sure how it got downstairs, but now it is on the kitchen table and it's spinning.

"I went to get some jars to bring some herbs in case we needed some, and when I came back in, it flew right in my face. I tried to grab it, but I dropped the bottles." Alek bent down to start picking up the glass. The marigold stopped spinning and drifted down. I caught it in my palm and examined it. It hadn't sung since the first day, although I was told it started spinning off and on when I was unconscious.

"I wonder what else it wants," I said while starting to unfold it. "Maybe there's more on the inside," I said mostly to myself. I folded and unfolded each flap, but there was nothing there. I shoved it into my pocket. It was a mystery for another time.

"Alright well, I'm ready to go. Where's Josephine?"

"She went to get some supplies from the garden; she'll be back in here shortly." I helped Alek with the rest of the glass and then we sat in the living room waiting for her to return. Once everything was packed away, she created the portal and we stepped through.

"Home sweet home," I said bitterly once we had made our way through the other side. It was bright and sunny. We landed right by the garden Kai and I spent most of our time in. It was hard not to allow the memories to flood back.

The uneasiness of being here made my skin start to itch. We needed to find my parents and fast. "Alright, Maven, so where is this so-called garden."

I turned toward my best friend just in time to see the uneasiness in her eyes before she shrouded it away. I had almost forgotten that she was about to be face to face with the man who killed her mother and father. Shit, this wasn't going to be easy on any of us.

"Well, I didn't actually see the garden itself. I heard the servants talking about it and when I tried to follow them, they disappeared. I don't think they even realized I was there."

"Goddesses," I said, sighing and rubbing my temples. "So, you don't even know where it is. We are on borrowed time, and we aren't going to be able to search every inch of these grounds. We might as well go back."

My jacket began to shake at the same moment as the origami marigold tried to fight its way out of my pocket. When it finally burst free, it spun in place and then began to move in the direction of Charlotte's cottage.

They immediately began to follow it. I had some reservations, but they didn't give me a chance to even voice them.

"Sure, let's just all blindly follow a spinning flower," I grumbled as I trudged behind them. It led us around the back of the cottage into the forest beyond it. A stone walking path had been put in so that Charlotte could take night walks without having to go through the grass, especially during the spring when it rained and got muddy. The marigold kept to the path, spinning faster and faster. The orange and yellow quickly became nothing more than a blur. As we followed it deeper into the forest, I realized I hadn't heard any noise outside of our footsteps crunching on the gravel. There were no birds chirping, no rustling of leaves as animals scattered to and fro; it was just eerie, ominous silence. This wasn't a path you walked to be around nature. This was like a walk to your death. Several miles in its depths, the marigold stopped abruptly.

Just as I was about to ask *what now*, a soft voice came from the other side of the brush.

"You're not supposed to be here, Princess."

"Who are you and how do you know me?" I charged into the bush as I asked. On the other side was a large clearing. There was a pond at the center of the clearing, completely covered in a thick white mist.

I could barely make out what looked like a small boat and a tiny house in the distance.

"Who are you?" I asked again. Josephine and the others came beside me, and we all looked out, trying to find where the voice had come from.

Out of the mist, a figure began to appear. No more than four feet tall, it was a small woman with greyish-blue skin and vibrant green eyes. "My name is Elecdora, I am a water nymph, and I am the protector of Kalen's Garden."

"So, you knew my father then?" I say.

"Yes, I did. I served the crown for many years. King Kalen was the nicest King I had ever had the pleasure of serving, and when he was imprisoned here, I asked Queen Charlotte to allow me to remain as his protector."

"So, they are here, my parents." I started to look around, thinking they would just appear out of the mist as well.

"They were, yes."

Charlotte
the night of the party

Maybe I had gone too far. Sariyah and I fought, but she had never been this angry. *She is getting bold though*, I thought to myself with a chuckle. She must really love that boy to openly threaten a Queen even If I was just holding her place until she asked for it.

She would understand one day. Everything I had done was for her. Well, not just for her, but for the sake of the kingdom. If Kalen is allowed to roam free, he will be the end of us all. His actions will surely invoke war and so many more will die.

How did I not see how power-hungry he was? Sofia as well. Those two were perfect for each other in the worst way. From the moment they announced their engagement, I knew they would be trouble. I just never imagined it would be this sort.

I should have paid more attention. I should have taken less trips and stayed closer to home. Maybe I could have prevented this.

"Oh well," I said aloud. "Nothing we can do about it now."

"Nothing we can do about what, Your Highness?" my servant Izzie came stepping out of the shadows. I had forgotten she was there.

"Oh, nothing, just the musings of an old woman with lots of regrets."

"With all due respect, Your Highness, you're not that old."

"The duties of being a queen can definitely age you, my dear," I said, still thinking about the mistakes of the past. So many things I wish I could do differently.

"May I ask you a question, Your Highness?" She looked at me with worried eyes.

"Go ahead," I told her, interested in what she had to ask.

"You don't think the princess meant what she said, do you? That she would really hurt you. I know it couldn't be easy to lose her boyfriend like that, but to question the Queen, to threaten the Queen? That is treason."

"My niece probably meant what she said. However, I don't think she would actually act on it. As angry as she might be, she knows she may not like my decisions, she may not even accept them, but she will follow them. That is, until she becomes queen herself."

"Who knows, maybe this will be the kick in the ass she needs to finally take over," I said with a wink. *I could only hope*, I added silently.

"That is good to know My Queen. I haven't met Princess Sariyah yet, but I've seen her and her handsome man around. I know she must be hurting. To give up that, he must have had a good reason." Izzie looked at me expectantly. I really didn't know how to answer. For this plan to work, everything had to be on a need-to-know basis.

So instead of confirming what was more of a statement than a question, I made my way into the throne room instead. The magical link Aryana had put inside me had started to hum. Which meant my visitor would be on their way soon.

"Izzie dear, I have a favor to ask."

"Anything for you, My Queen," she said eagerly.

"There may come a time where my niece will need a friend. She may feel like all is lost and be on the verge of giving up. You will know when that time comes. I ask that you be a friend to her. Be an ear to hear her troubles and just show her kindness and grace. Remind her that I love her and that the people love her and that she will be an amazing queen if only she could not be so stubborn."

"Of course, Your Highness. I will do whatever I can to help the Princess, but I have to say, this sounds more like a goodbye than a request. Do you plan on leaving court for a while?"

"I really don't know where the future will take me; for now though, I could really use some tea. Would you be a dear and fetch some for me?"

"Yes, Your Highness." Izzie bowed and rushed away to the kitchen. Hopefully, it took her a minute to get back. My guest had arrived, and I did not want to be interrupted.

"Hello Brother. Come out of the shadows, will you?"

"You look good on that throne, little sister, almost like it belonged to you instead of being stolen." Kalen walked into the middle of the room to face me. He managed to change out of the rags he had been left to rot in and instead donned an impeccable suit. Completely in black, which was his favorite color. He looked like he belonged to the night itself.

"It was fairly easy to get in here, don't tell me you are having trouble paying the guards," he teased. "I left the court with a small fortune that should have been enough."

"Well," I said with a bite of venom in my voice, "knowing you had a penchant for murdering indiscriminately, I thought it's best to give them the night off."

"Ah, so you knew then I would break free from your little cage; must have been that pesky oracle of yours. Got to remember to kill her as soon as I'm done here." He laughed with so much hate in his voice it sent shivers down my spine.

How could my brother have fallen so far? As kid, he always had grandiose ideas. He was the person I looked up to the most. So many times, he had protected me, helped me, and loved me. But now, the man I see before me doesn't even come close to the brother I knew.

"It hurt me, you know," I tell him. "When I found out it was you who was behind everything, it hurt me to my core. My niece, your daughter, had been one of those children you were hell-bent on slaughtering, and I refused to believe you would do anything to hurt her. But then I saw them; I saw the bodies of the children you killed. It was then that I knew that it had to be me to stop you. I had to make sure you never caused any more harm."

"I didn't want to hurt her," he said, moving forward towards me. "I tried everything I could. I tried to remove her powers and that did not work. I had to bind them instead. Even that couldn't contain it. Day by day, she grew stronger, even with the spell placed on her. She would have the power to take my throne before I was ready to relinquish it, if I was ever ready to.

"I worked too hard little sister, I clawed my way to the top and I'm not going to let anyone, not even my flesh and blood, take what's rightfully mine away from me."

He was less than three feet away from me now. It was just as Aryana foresaw.

Quick as the panther he shifts into, he was upon me. He grabbed me by my throat so quickly I didn't have time to react. Not that I would have. Everything must go as it should.

"You should have done more than stop me dear sister; you should have killed me."

With that, he shoved his now-clawed hand right through my chest.

Surrounded and Afraid

"What do you mean were?" I growled, stepping towards the nymph. "Where are they?"

"Sariyah, relax."

"Relax? How can I relax? We risked a lot coming here and now she's saying they aren't here!?" I swiveled around to face my friends. "Do you know what this means? If they aren't in here, that means they are out somewhere in the world, probably creating chaos."

"Master Kalen would never," the nymph started to say. I glared back at her, daring her to continue the lie.

She was trembling; I could see the tears forming in her eyes. Goddess, whatever lies my father fed her must have been coated in gold the way she was clinging to them.

"I know what they said about him," she said, starting to regain some of her earlier confidence. "He would never. It was a misunderstanding. He is a good man. I have been here every day for the last 14 years. I watched Master Kalen and Queen Sofia. He told me the lies his sister was spreading, making it seem like he was a monster when all he was doing was protecting us. With their powers left unchecked, those people would have been the end of us."

"Those children, you mean." Maven stepped forward to meet her gaze. "Those children were seven years old, and they didn't deserve to die because of two people's undeniable greed.

And it wasn't just children they killed. They killed anyone who got in their way, including my mother."

"You're wrong! All of you are wrong." As Elecdora began to shout, the mist around us began to swirl around her. This was the power of a water nymph, able to manipulate any form of water, even the molecules that make up mist. The more she cried out, the more the mist cocooned around her as if it was protecting her. The upside was that as it pooled around her, it began to clear and we could see more of the clearing. I looked back at Elecdora, who was now in a fetal position inside her mist bubble. I felt bad for her. I am all too aware of how it feels to have the image of someone you love be shattered.

"That must have been where they were kept." I can hear Josephine speaking from ahead. A doorway had appeared almost out of thin air. Or maybe I just wasn't paying attention. The frame was splintered around the edges as if the door that should have been there had burst at the seams. Or that something had burst through it.

It was dark and cold in the room. The sunlight from the clearing stopping just at the entryway, as if it too was afraid of what was inside. I peered inside, eager to see what my parents had been living in. As my eyes adjusted to the darkness, I was able to see the room. It was roughly twelve feet by twelve feet. If there was a window, it would have been on the door that is now missing. The steel walls were covered in claw marks as if a beast had gone crazy in here, lashing out haphazardly. There was one large bed in one corner and a toilet in the other. Aside from a tray on the bed, there was nothing else in the room. No clothing, no books, no paper, nothing, just a lingering air of despair and hate. Shuddering, I left the room, squeezing past Maven and Alek, who had also come to inspect the quarters.

Josephine was kneeling down near the nymph, softly speaking to her in an effort to comfort her.

I stared long and hard at her before speaking. Normally I would have gone with a more diplomatic approach, but we were running out of time.

"Tell me where they are." I said, enunciating each word fiercely. "Where are my parents; when did they get out."

"I don't know," she sniffled. "It's just like I told the other lady. One minute it was quiet and then the next minute, a giant panther came bursting out of the door, followed by a jet-black wolf with green eyes. It had to be Kalen and Sofia. They raced off into the woods."

"Another woman?" Who could she be. "Well, that isn't as important right now. How did they get free and why did you not stop them?"

"I don't know how they got free; you'd have to ask your aunt; I'm surprised she hasn't come down here yet to berate me. As for master Kalen, I was here only to protect him. I was his friend, not his guard."

"This woman you said came here. What did she look like?"

"She had olive skin and brown hair. It was braided down her back in several rows. She had very pretty eyes. I had never seen purple irises before."

"When did she come? When did my parents get free."

"She came a few days after they left. It was several months ago."

"Several months ago? Do you remember what day?" I knew the answer before she even spoke it. My head started spinning and I wanted to throw up. If they had gotten free when I think they did, then the answer to the biggest question had been answered.

"It was the day of Charlotte 's party."

And there it was, the final bomb being dropped on any hope I had. My parents killed my aunt and framed me for it. I didn't have enough time to swallow that bile in my throat before I heard it.

Footsteps, and a lot of them. The royal guard had found us again.

"Mave, Alek," I yelled out, but it was unnecessary; they were already at my side.

"What do you want to do Sai, fight or run?" Alek and Josephine were poised to create a portal and

Maven looked like she could knock a few heads together.

Looking at my friends ready to go to war for me or go back on the run, I felt an overwhelming amount of love. This was my true family.

I couldn't ask them to follow me this time. I needed something far more important. "I am going to stand trial," I told them grimly.

"I'm done running. We have found enough evidence to hopefully clear my name."

"Sariyah, you can't do this; what if they kill you before you have a chance to even defend yourself?"

I felt his presence behind me, but I had already sensed him coming. Sandalwood and lavender, my two favorite scents. One minute there was nothing and the next, I was engulfed in it. There were no magic tricks this time. He came out in the open with probably a hundred guards. All outfitted with weapons and armor. I turned around to face him,

"All this for little ol' me?" I said, poking him squarely in the chest.

"Let's be honest; it would take far more than this to make you even break a sweat. I'm hoping you play nicely."

I flash my fangs and make eye contact with as many guards as I can. I want them to understand that I am not going down. I am coming willingly.

"Sariyah, can we trust him?" Mave said. "After all, he knew all of this and said nothing. Not only that, but he spearheaded this witch hunt. For lack of a better word."

Kai looked up to meet her eyes. I could see the tense exchange between both of them. My protectors both wanted to keep me out of harm's way

"It's okay guys, besides, like I said, you have something more important to do. Nothing I say during my trial will mean anything without witnesses and proof. Round up everyone you can to speak on my behalf, anyone who will speak about my parents and the horrors they inflicted."

"If anything happens to her Kai. If one hair on her head is removed, I promise I will kill you myself." I had never heard Alek speak so frankly. Especially not to Kai. All of the charming, bad-boy flirtatiousness was gone, and before me stood a lethal warrior.

"She won't die Alek," Kai said gruffly. "I'd sooner die myself than let anything happen to her."

"Alright, as scintillating as this conversation is, we all have somewhere to be," I said halfheartedly. "You guys have your work cut out for you, and I have a jail cell calling my name."

Alek, Maven, Josephine, and the wood nymph Elecdora quickly went through the portal. At the last-minute, Alek turned around and mouthed *I'll kill you* and threw an obscene gesture at Kai, and just like that, they were gone.

"Goddess," Kai said, rolling his eyes, "why is he so dramatic."

"Probably because he feels just as betrayed as I do." I don't try to hide the pain or the anger in my voice. As I look at him, I can't help but get angry all over again. It's like I am reliving that day in my head.

"I need you to put these on," he says, clearly dodging the statement. In his hands were a pair of silver cuffs. Each bracelet had runes carved into them. I had heard about these but never actually seen them. They were forged by the best locksmiths in Alexandria and imbued with magic to keep anyone from using magic once they were closed. In my case, it would keep me from shifting.

"Seriously? I scoff. "Now, who's being dramatic." I hold my wrists out so he can put them on. His fingers slightly brush against my skin, and it is electric. As much as I don't want to want him, my body betrays me every time. I would be lying if I said I didn't miss his touch. He rubbed his thumb along the center of my palm, the heat from my body coming to my head there as if it was a beacon drawing everything out of me. The look in his eyes was anything but professional. Standing this close to him, I could almost imagine what it would be like to have him take me right here in this field. His lips turned up into a sexy smirk that had my face heating up.

"I know what you're thinking" he said, dropping my hands. "However, I don't think these warriors would like that kind of show."

Shit, I thought silently. I had forgotten they were even there. "Trust me, it would have been the greatest part of their night," I said defiantly, matching his grin. I walked toward the edge of the clearing from which we came, Kai followed close behind. He ordered the guards to flank on either side and we made our way out of the forest. I walked painfully slow, trying to enjoy each moment of freedom. I could hear the Royal Guards grumbling, urging Kai to make me walk faster. He quieted them with a glance. He understood what I was walking into, and he was more than happy to oblige.

Sins of the Father

"Sariyah Marie Devereaux, you stand accused of the murder of Queen Regent Charlotte Devereaux."

"How do you plead. "

"Not guilty, Your Honors." The council members that were remaining wasted no time. As soon as we cleared the forest and passed my old house, they were already waiting. I was rushed straight to the castle and into the Council's quarters. They made Kai leave, stating that his duties were done. He tried to protest, but I gave him a silent okay.

"I will be fine," I said with a nod. He looked at them one more time, looking like he wanted to argue further, but he turned away and slammed the door.

The door opened again and I was ready to yell at Kai but instead walked in a different Gerard. This is definitely where Kai got his looks. Swaggering over to the desk where the three other council members sat was none other than Marcel Gerard. Kai's father.

"I hope I'm not too late. Word had only just gotten to me that the traitor had finally been apprehended, by my son, nonetheless. So, have we decided how we are going to kill her? My vote is for beheading in the courtyard." He said it so nonchalantly, as if he was talking about what he wanted for dinner rather than my demise.

"Goddess above Marcel, could you be more crude?" The person coming to my defense was Regina Salvatore. She was one of two witches on the council. There were five seats altogether. There was a seat for the reigning vampire, a seat for the reigning werewolf, and a seat for the reigning shifter. There were two seats for the witches as they spoke, not just for themselves but for the remaining creatures who did not want to be bothered by the politics, including goblins, nymphs, fairies etc.

The other witch on the council was Freya Dubois. The only seats unoccupied were King Charles and, of course, my late aunt.

"The child killed her aunt, Regina; this is no time for pleasantries. I suggest we kill her and move on. After all, there is still the matter of a new crowning."

He didn't even try to hide his glee. With me out of the way and Charlotte dead, the Gerard's were finally able to take back what they felt was their rightful place at the head of the crown.

"I'm right here, you know." I said loudly to garner his attention. "The murdering traitor is less than 20 feet away; you could at least stop addressing me as if I weren't here."

"Child, I shall do as I please. You're lucky that ignoring your presence is all that I do. For your crimes against the crown and for how you toyed with my son, you're lucky that I don't kill you where you sit."

"Kill me," I said, snarling right back. "You couldn't kill me even with these cuffs on. The only thing that would happen is another Gerard losing to another Devereaux woman."

Granted, my mother was not a Devereaux when she beat Marcel's grandpa, but it didn't matter. The pure implication was enough to set Marcel's eyes ablaze. He was almost foaming at the mouth.

"You insolent little bitch," he spat. "You know nothing about the power of the Gerard's. Your mother was little more than a whore. She didn't earn the title; she fucked her way to it."

"Enough of this!" Freya stood up from her seat, her purple dress swaying furiously at the abrupt movement. "Sir Marcel, if you cannot be professional, then the least you can do is keep your mouth shut," she said, turning her gaze to him. "There was absolutely no need for you to come in and insult the prisoner and waste our time with talks about a seat you're not even qualified to sit on."

"Damn," I said, chuckling. "Even the witches don't like you."

"It is only at the behest of the Royal Guard Captain that we are giving you this preliminary meeting. He seems to think this is what the late Queen would have wanted. He has pleaded your innocence even after being instructed to bring you in; dead or alive. The fact that you did not kill the guards who were sent to capture you and instead sent them back beaten and bruised has also played a role in our decision."

The angry *hmph* from Marcel let me know this was not a unanimous decision.

"I am grateful Your Honors." Suffice to say; Kai was definitely in my head. Here he was protecting me like always. Even when the rest of Court probably didn't think I deserved it. I'm sure he got a ton of heat for it. Judging from the look in his father's eyes, he was probably going to get a lot more.

"I appreciate this opportunity more than you know. I didn't kill my aunt; I was framed."

"Then why did you run?" Regina asked. "You fled the Court before we could even ask any questions."

"She told me to. I had come to her room to apologize for my earlier outburst. I wanted to ask her why she did this and explain why it hurt; I hoped I would be able to change her mind about forcing Kai onto her Royal Guard. When I got to the throne room, she had already been attacked. Someone or something had gone through a portal moments before, and I couldn't do anything to stop it."

This was the first time I had spoken about Charlotte's death. Even as I told my side, I couldn't help but allow the tears to finally flow. "I loved my aunt; I truly did. It didn't matter how much we fought or argued; whenever I needed her, she was there. Not as Queen Regent but just as my aunt."

I felt a hand on my shoulder. A servant had come to offer me tissues. I was a blubbering snotty mess. She squeezed my shoulder and dashed back behind the council members.

I wiped away the tears and blew my nose before finally continuing

"I didn't heed her warning at first. I was confused and hurt. The next day, I heard you were looking for me and that the guards had come forward about the threat I made at dinner the night before."

"The threat of killing her that you made just a few hours before she was found dead if I'm not mistaken." This time it was Freya who spoke. Her words not so much an accusation but rather an attempt to fill in the blanks.

"That's correct, Councilwoman Freya," I said, returning the respect she has shown me by using her full title.

"After learning that you thought I was the one to blame, I panicked. I thought you were the ones she was trying to warn me about. That maybe there had been a coup amongst the Council and that I was going to be killed as well. So, I ran. I didn't look back and I don't regret it."

"Were you ever able to get a lead on who you thought framed you?" Regina asked.

"Yes, I did. It was my father." I met each pair of eyes so they could tell I was serious. I understood the implications of what I was saying.

"Your father died, child. Do you really expect us to believe he came back from the dead to kill his little sister? What would be his motive?"

"My father didn't have to come back from the dead because he never actually died. He and my mother have been imprisoned since that day. That's where the Royal Guard found us today. We came to get information from them, but they had broken out. Presumably, the day of the graduation party."

"But why," Marcel pressed on, "why would Kalen want to kill his sister, why was he imprisoned as you say, and why did the Queen Regent lie to us?" Something about his questions felt off to me. Almost like he already knew the answers but wanted to ask them anyway. If that was the case, his face didn't let on.

"Because of the prophecy." It was Freya who answered.

Trial or Death?

"What prophecy," Regina asked, turning towards her. "I haven't heard about any prophecies in a long time."

"That's because this one was hushed from the very beginning. Several years ago, an oracle from my village had a prophecy. There would be children born under a reaping moon who would have enhanced powers that would rival that of even the crown. Those children would bring about a new era and eventually, one of them would open a gate allowing the goddesses to return to this realm. The oracle had brought up to the Council of that time and was casted out. Years later, when the reaping moon came, she once again tried to warn the people. You hadn't been sworn in Regina, so you weren't there. But I was and so were Kalen, Sofia, and

Charles. The only one who really believed her was Charles. That was until seven years later when the children started to go missing."

"I still don't believe that nonsense," Marcel said from his seat. He lounged back, not bothering to look like he had any interest in being here. Which was a stark contrast from when he came in screaming for my head.

"That Oracle was a bloody fool. Speaking nothing but nonsense."

"Josephine," Freya said through clenched teeth, "is anything but. Not only is she an Oracle, but she is also a gifted witch. She helped so many in my village with her potions and herbs. I have no reason to believe she would lie. If Charles were here, he would say the same."

"I still don't understand," Regina cut in, shooting both of the council members an icy stare, reminding them this was official business. "What does the prophecy have to do with Kalen, Sofia, and Charlotte?"

"Long story short, Councilwoman Regina, my parents were behind the deaths of those children, as they feared what that would mean for their rule. My Aunt Charlotte found out and imprisoned them with the help of a witch. I don't I know why she hid it from everyone, and unfortunately, she was killed before we could get an answer."

"Where is your father now," Councilwoman Regina asked.

"I honestly don't know. Probably somewhere kicking puppies and planning his next child massacre."

I could see the confusion on her face. She didn't know whether to believe me or sentence me to death. I couldn't afford it to be the latter, so I spoke quickly.

"I don't have my parents, but I do have evidence and witnesses that will attest that what I am saying is true. If I could just have some more time for them to arrive, I am sure we will be able to present you with all the evidence."

Marcel and Freya looked to Regina. Her face was a stern unreadable mask. "I am in favor of hearing her out," Freya said, finally breaking the silence.

"I am in favor of killing her right now," Marcel said with a glint in his eyes. That nagging feeling that something wasn't right about him returned. I never really spoke to him while Kai and I dated, so there was no real justification for his apparent hate of me. Other than the fact that I am the daughter of the woman he feels stole his crown. But it's something else eating at me. No one should be this cruel. I didn't have time to ponder any longer. Regina stood up.

"We still need to discuss this with Charles as he couldn't get here in time. Once a decision is made, you will be notified. I will have the guards take you to your rooms. Traitor or not, you are still a princess, and I will not have you laying in a dungeon." At that, she briskly walked out the door. Marcel quickly followed her, probably to try and convince her to kill me. That just left me, Councilwoman Freya, and the servant girl alone in the room.

"Your aunt was more than just a Councilwoman," Freya said, rising, "she was my friend. I really hope her killer is brought to justice," as she walked by me, she squeezed my shoulder firmly, and then she too was gone.

After a few minutes, a gruff guard came to collect me to take me to my room. The servant girl had apparently been given the job of taking care of me while I was in custody, so she followed behind. She was quiet and very meek. Her mousy brown hair tucked into a neat bun. She barely made eye contact with anyone, just skittered around, trying to stay out of sight when not needed. The room he led me to wasn't my actual room, rather just a room in the castle. I had rarely been here since we never really used it and I would rather train with the warriors than do politics. I was surprised by how updated everything was. The room itself was pretty large. When you enter, it has its own living room area and a balcony overlooking one of the gardens. The bed was massive and covered in pillows. The duvet was a beautiful cream color with lace applique. Adjacent to the bed was an enormous walk-in closet that also led you to the bathroom. As far as prisons go, this was definitely top-notch. The guard removed the handcuffs when we came into the room, but there must have been magical wards in place as I still could not shift. I could feel my wolf just beneath the skin, but my power was muted. I couldn't even bring my claws out if I wanted to.

It was still pretty early in the afternoon, the sunlight peeking through the wide window. I could see the servants bustling about. I could even see an annoying number of guards stationed here for "my protection." I really didn't know what to do. I couldn't exactly relax as the council debated over my future. I hope Maven and Alek aren't having a challenging time convincing people to come to my aid. "Goddesses," I said aloud, pushing myself onto the bed knocking a few pillows to the floor. I hope this isn't for naught.

"Princess Sariyah." At the sound of the voice, I nearly jumped out of my skin. I had thought the servant girl had left and I didn't hear any footsteps, yet there she was moving as quiet as a mouse. "I don't mean to disturb you, but you have a visitor and lunch. Shall I have them come back?"

"No, no, it's fine," I said, pushing myself up on my elbows. "I'm hungry anyways, and I would love to see who was brave enough to come visit the murderous traitor."

I had thought the servant would tense up at me, calling myself that, but instead, she chuckled and went to open the door. *At least she has a good sense of humor,* I thought to myself.

"Captain Kai, the princess will see you," she said, holding the door open. As Kai stepped inside, she stepped around him and gave me a wink, moving just as quietly as before.

"Of course, you would come here," I said, rolling my eyes. He stood there with a large rectangular tray in his hand, the smells wafting from it, making my mouth water.

"I could always leave," he said with that annoyingly sexy smile. "I mean, if you're not hungry." He started to turn to the door as if he were really going to leave.

"You wouldn't dare leave a starving prisoner!" I said fake pouting. "How would that look to our neighboring allies. The shifter court treated their prisoners like slaves. I can only imagine the uproar."

He turns back, pretending to ponder the accusations. "Hmm, you're absolutely correct; that would definitely look bad on us."

He sets the tray on the bed and takes a step back. I fully look at him this time. He has changed out of the normal black and red warrior gear and has opted for a fitted white t-shirt and skinny beige jeans. His dreads are pulled back neatly into a low ponytail. He smiles nervously as I look him over. Even with all our bantering, there is still too much to say and neither of us is ready to begin.

I grab the tray and take the lid off, choosing to focus on the food instead of the unspoken feelings. Yum, beef stew and fresh-baked bread. One of my favorite meals. I rip a chunk off of the loaf of bread, dip it into the stew and shove the whole piece in my mouth. It's not the most ladylike display, but it's what I have become accustomed to after being on the run for so long—having to eat our meals quickly and then be on the go so we could always remain one step ahead of whoever was looking for us.

Kai watched me in silence as I scarfed down the remaining food. I tried to slow down and really enjoy it. This could be my last meal and I deserved to actually enjoy it. As soon as the last of the stew was gone, Kai took the tray and set it on the table before coming back and sitting on the edge of the bed.

"It wouldn't be too much to ask for dessert," I said, laying back into the pillows. The best and worst part of eating comfort food was the drowsiness that came with it. Everything around me seemed to move slowly and my body felt heavy as it sank into the welcoming embrace of the soft mattress. Before I shut my eyes, I heard Kai whisper that he would make sure I got dessert later, after that, everything went dark.

I slept peacefully for the first time in ages. You would think that knowing I could get word of my death at any moment would have me tangled up in knots, but I was blissfully at peace. Come what may, I was going to enjoy the little things while I could.

When I awoke, the sun had begun to set. There was a note on my beside table next to a silver tray, smaller than the one Kai used for lunch. After a small inner debate, I opted for the tray first. Just in case, whatever was inside that note made me lose my appetite.

I pulled the little tray into my lap and uncovered it. Sitting inside were three pink cupcakes with pink buttercream frosting: Strawberry on Strawberry, my absolute favorite. I squealed with delight. I always had to special request them from the cooks because no one else ate them, which in all honesty, is their loss. Bringing my favorite food definitely gives Kai some brownie points, but if he thinks this makes up for everything, he's got another thing coming. I take a bite of one of the cupcakes and open up the note. It's in Kai's handwriting.

Sariyah, hope you enjoy your desserts, the cooks were very happy to make them. Looks like you still have some loyal subjects here despite everything.

The Council finished deliberating while you napped. I asked that they not disturb you. Your formal trial will be held in three days' time. Your friends will have been notified by the time you read this as well as the rest of the courts. At my father's request, it will be held out in the courtyard so that our subjects can also attend. I am doing everything in my power to make sure you make it out of this.

I love you, Sariyah. And I always will.

Kai

Well, I'm certainly glad I ate the cupcake first.

Lovers Quarrel

The next two days went by painfully slow. Kai was busy preparing for my trial and also had to tend to his duties as Captain. He did manage to have notes sent to me and after dinner, I always had strawberry on strawberry cupcakes. I wasn't allowed to leave my room and there was no one here who would visit. I spent most of the days staring out the window, sleeping, or complaining to my servant about how much this sucked. I found out her name was Izzie. She was a shifter as well, her form being, I kid you not, a mouse. No wonder she moved so damn quietly. She completed training and graduated a few years ahead of me and decided not to stay in the military. Her mother was a servant to my aunt and she really enjoyed the work. She would come and bring me my meals as well as my notes from Kai. See to it that I bathed and brushed my hair.

She would sometimes let things slip about her personal life, like her boyfriend who lived in the city and how she had hoped this would be the year he proposes. Other than that, it was just business as usual.

That evening when she brought me my dinner (the cooks really out-did themselves this time. Smothered pork chops, cabbage, and bacon with rice and, of course, cornbread), my tray of treats was missing.

When I asked about them, she giggled and just said that the captain wanted to bring them himself.

I didn't bother to hide my excitement. I pretty much spent the last two hours convincing myself that I am living in my last days so that my hopes would already be low should things not go my way.

"Kai is coming? Do you know when?" She purposely acted as if she did not hear me. I stared at her; she moved around the room, cleaning imaginary dust off of objects just to let the dramatic pause build.

"Izzie, I am going to explode. Would you please let me know when my ex-boyfriend will be here?" I tried not to growl, but she was really trying my patience in a good way. Maven would love her, and Alek would probably try to bed her. This wasn't the first time I thought about my friends. I missed them dearly even though it had only been three days. We had been on the run together for five months and were together almost every day before that. My heart ached when I thought about not possibly seeing them. I shook the thought out of my head and returned my attention to Izzie, who still had not spilled the proverbial beans.

"Come on Izzie; I'm cooped up in this room, probably going to die tomorrow. Are you really going to make me wait?"

"Has anyone told you that you're dramatic Princess?" she said it so sassily with one hand on her hip, I had no choice but to snort with laughter.

"I may have been told that a time or two," I said between chuckles. "But I have also been called spoiled, impatient, and above all deadly...so if you would be so kind."

"Ohhh," she said mockingly. "Am I supposed to be afraid of the big bad wolf? In this room without your powers, I'm sure even I could take you." The look in her eyes told me she was serious. After all, she went through the same training I did.

"So, if threatening and begging won't work, what about a bribe?" I teased. "If you tell me when he is coming so that I can prepare, I'll make you the head of the servants when I become queen."

"If you don't die tomorrow," she said with a cackle.

I feigned hurt and pretend-clutched my pearls. "Wow, who knew you could be so mean," I said. "But yes, should I not be beheaded tomorrow, the job is yours."

"Well then, he will be here in an hour," she said with a smile. "That should be just enough time for you to finish your dinner, take a bath, and put on something other than sweats and a tank top." As she spoke, she looked me up and down. She had brought me clothes the first night, but I wanted to be comfy in my prison, so I never wore any of the dresses.

"That is not enough time," I said. "Had you told me when I first asked, I would have had like 20 more minutes!" I hurriedly finished my food as she started my bath. Goddess above, I don't know what I would do if he got here too soon.

Just as Izzie finished braiding the single braid down my back, I heard a soft knock on the door.

"Well, that's my cue to leave." Izzie sauntered to the door and curtsied to Kai as she left the room. "Have fun you two," she said with a laugh.

"What does she mean by that?" Kai said with a puzzled look on his face.

I sat in the middle of the bed, picking at the loose threads of the blanket. "Who knows, she's a weird girl," I said, trying to hide my eagerness. I had an idea of what he wanted to talk about, but I also hoped we wouldn't talk at all.

I heard him set the tray on the table next to the bed and take his seat on the corner. I heard the sounds of plates being moved around and then suddenly, there was one being slid into my lap. In the center was, of course, a cupcake.

I greedily unwrapped it and took a bite, closing my eyes with pure delight. It was really heaven on earth. I do not know how something so sweet could elicit such a reaction, but I'm fairly sure the chefs made these with some love potion because they tasted even better than normal.

When I opened my eyes, Kai was looking at me with a sly smile.

"What?" I asked.

He reached over and wiped of the icing off of my lip with his thumb. He then proceeded to lick it off his thumb in a sinfully ungentlemanly manner.

His eyes slid down to my dress, where I am sure two peaks were pushing against the silk of the dress. I immediately regretted my choice. I wanted something sexy yet casual and decided on a thin, pink number that looked enchanting against my brown skin. But now I'm wishing I had just put on a t-shirt and maybe a damn bra.

His fingers started to twitch slightly, relaying what was clearly on his mind. I had almost hoped he would reach out and caresses them. Instead, he forced himself to make eye contact with me and cleared his throat, scooting a little farther away as if he could feel the heat radiating off me.

"We should talk," he said, his voice straining behind his passion.

"Talk about what exactly, you betraying me, ending our engagement, joining the Royal Guard, sleeping with some witch when I had only been gone for a few months, or the secrets you and my aunt held from me for goddess knows how long?"

"I didn't sleep with her." In true male fashion, he bypassed everything else I said and only answered a single part of the question. Not going to lie though, I was happy with his answer.

"Yeah sure," I said, not willing to give him an inch. "You should have heard the way Alek talked about her; you would have thought she was a goddess. She probably wasn't even all that cute."

"Sariyah, I didn't sleep with her. I haven't been with anyone since you left. As for all your other accusations, yes, those are what I wanted to talk about."

He actually looked hurt and a little offended that I thought he would be with someone else.

"Well, who is she then, and why did you never tell me about her."

"I didn't know about her until the night before graduation. Even if I did, I couldn't say anything. Queen Charlotte swore me to secrecy. A few months before graduation, she told me about the prophecy; I had already known parts of it as my parents told me when I was younger. They left out the part where your dad was murdering kids. However, they told me to hold back my strength until I got older so as not to arouse any suspicion. Charlotte told me the full truth though. She also told me that an Oracle came to see her earlier that day. Told her that in a month's time, the wards holding King Kalen would fall and that he would come to kill her."

I was at a loss for words. Sensing that, he continues.

"She knew she was going to die, and she knew that there was a chance your father would come for you too. So, she prepared. The oracle who came to visit her was the same witch Alek would have seen in Maven's memories. She is extremely powerful and I'm quite sure she was the witch who helped Queen Charlotte trap Kalen the first time. That's why I pressed Alek to practice mind walking and that why I sparred with Maven so often, I had to make sure they were strong enough to protect you and to help you when the time came." He kept going on, but I could barely hear him, something he said triggered me and I couldn't let it go.

"So you knew for six months this was going to happen," I said, cutting him off. "Six whole months and you still asked me to marry you. You asked me to marry you, knowing you would have to join the Royal Guard and break my heart. You sat there for months, lying to my face. We planned a future together, Malikai." In all my years of knowing him, I had never used his given name. I was so angry and so hurt I said it without even thinking.

"Everything else I don't like that you lied about, but I can understand. For the sake of the battle, sometimes things need to be secret. But how could you ask me for forever when you knew you wouldn't be able to keep it. That is cruel."

I could feel the tears running down my face, but I didn't wipe them away. This man was supposed to be my husband, my king, my forever and a day, as we liked to say. And he lied to me.

"How the hell did that fit into Charlotte's plan? Did she think leaving me broken would keep me from coming back here and having my dad murder me too?"

"No, she didn't even know. It had nothing to do with any of this. I had already been planning to ask you. I meant everything I said when I proposed, and I meant everything that we planned after. Hell, if we can make it through your trial, your dad, and this damn prophecy, I want to make good on all of those promises.

"I love you Sariyah Marie Devereaux. I will love you until I take my last breath and then I will love you even after. I know I fucked up and I know I hurt you and I am sorry. I think in my own messed up way, I thought if I still proposed to you, then that would somehow make sure that everything would turn out right." He spoke with so much passion. Even as angry as I was, it was beautiful to see him be so open and vulnerable with me.

He looked so nervous despite the confidence in his voice. His hands now twisting in his lap as he spoke, trying to make sense of his decisions. I had already forgiven him. From the moment he said he would love me forever, whatever anger I held against him dissipated. The only thing left was my love for him.

I pulled him over to me, falling back into the bed so that he was right above me. Then I kissed him. The moment my lips found his, my body lit on fire. He deepened the kiss, forcing me to open my mouth and let his tongue explore and caress mine. I could feel my body responding to him; the peaks in my dress appeared fully hardened. I could feel his body hardening too. I wrapped my legs around his waist, pulling him into me. I could feel the pressure against me, his hips rhythmically thrusting as if drawn to the heat between my legs. He pushed his way up and looked at me. "Are you sure you want to do this Sai?"

"Yes." Before I could even get the full word out, he shoved his hand under my dress, his fingers seeking out what was poking underneath. Once they found what they were looking for, he begin to circle around them. I let out a soft groan. I hadn't felt this kind of pleasure in a long time and clearly, neither had he. As my body began to arch towards him, he used that moment to rip the dress off me.

The way he looked at me with pure arousal made me shudder. There were no words to really express how I was feeling. It was like every second I didn't have him inside me was pure torture. I gripped the edge of his t-shirt and slid it up over his head. He bent down a little to make it easier on me—the tattoo on his chest is in full display. I traced over it with my finger. It was a beautiful wolf in the forest at night; there was the moon and the stars, and it finished down his arm with the goddess Luna on his bicep.

His body shuddered underneath my touch as if my finger were shooting lightning into him. I placed both my hands on his broad chest and caressed my way up until I held his face in them; I pulled him back down to me and kissed him with as much passion as I could muster. This time while we kissed, his finger began to trace the inside of my thigh, moving upward until he found the hem of the lace panties. Without removing his lips from mine, he arched up my lower half and slid them off. I was completely naked underneath him and completely at his mercy. As if he could read my thoughts, he brought his fingers back up my thighs, this time spreading them open. As he reached the apex, he slipped a finger inside of me as I groaned slightly. He pulled back to look at me once more, his finger still moving. With a sinister grin, he then thrust another finger inside while still rhythmically rubbing the apex. Goddess, I felt like I was going to explode. My groans only seemed to fuel him as he thrusted harder and further into me, and just when I was about to climax, he stopped.

My eyes shot open, but all I could do was whimper in protest. "Did you think I would let you off that easily," he said.

"Kai please," I began to mumble.

"Uh uh," he said, his voice deep and sultry. He pulled his fingers from me and I again whimpered. I didn't want him to stop, not when I had been so close. Just as I was opening my mouth to protest, he put his fingers right in my mouth. The same fingers that had just been inside me. The pure delight in his eyes as he made me taste myself almost sent me off the edge. I sucked each one of his fingers, slowly drawing it out. The bulge in his pants gets larger each time. I reached out my hands to unbutton his pants and release his manhood. Where some men had either length or girth, Kai had both. As soon as he was freed my hands were on him. I wanted to give him the same pleasure he gave me. I began stroking, slowly at first, starting at him in his eyes as he began to once against shudder under my touch. The more aroused he looked, the faster my fingers stroked. Now it was his turn to moan. Kai kept his eyes closed as his hands clenched the bed around us. I wiggled myself closer to his body. I angled my hips so that I could slip him inside me. Just the tip. He tried to move so that he was further inside me, but I pressed one hand on his chest. I wanted to tease him just as he had done me.

"Sariyah," he growled, breathless as I began to grind my hips. "You are wicked."

His mouth finds mine again, and in one swift motion, the hand that had been holding him at bay was now pinned above my head. His eyes were wide and gleaming with lust. The golden specks bright like pools of sunshine.

He pushed inside me, my body straining to allow every inch inside. "I love you," I gasped. It was the only thing I could think of to say. I could barely think at all. He thrust inside me, taking deep, slow strokes, each one eliciting more pleasure than the last.

"Say it again," he said. I'd scream it from the tallest tower if I had to.

"I love you Malikai Gerard; I love you." He thrust even faster now. The teasing was replaced with desire. I don't know how many times I said I love you to him or even how many times we found release, but the sun was beginning to rise by the time we stopped.

Return of the King

I curled up next to him, our bodies sweaty and exhausted.

"I don't want you to go," I crooned, tracing the stars on his chest. "I wish we could just skip town and forget about the trial." He laid there with his eyes closed, but his brow furrowed when I mentioned the trial as if he had forgotten.

"I don't want to go either. I promise you though, this was not the last time." He pulled me on top of him and kissed my forehead, and we lay like that for a little longer. I had almost fallen asleep on his chest when there was a knock on the door.

"Who the hell is visiting you this early," Kai said lazily. He must have been on the verge of sleep too.

"I don't know," I responded, my voice matching his. "Let's just pretend we didn't hear them. The trial isn't until this afternoon anyways; we have some time."

The door creaked open, and Kai snatched the blankets up over us. Now on alert, the sleepiness faded from his eyes.

"Who goes there," he growled menacingly.

"I am sorry to interrupt so early, Princess and Captain," Izzie said hesitantly from behind the cracked door. "But the Princess' friends have just arrived and are demanding to see her. I tried to tell them you were busy, but the vampire said, and I quote, 'Tell Kai to get his werewolf ass out of her bed and let us spend the morning with her."

At the mention of my friends, I was upright in the bed. Maven and Alek are here. I quickly untangled myself from Kai and began to make it to the door. Izzie's eyes widened as I went to move past her.

"Princess, don't you want to get dressed first?"

Kai howled with laughter, like, actually howled.

"I was almost hurt that you were so quick to leave me for your friends, but I would have paid good money to see the look on their faces when you ran out there naked. Besides, you're not allowed to leave this room remember?"

"Ah shit," I cursed. I was so excited I had forgotten both of those two important things.

"Why doesn't the captain run you a bath and I'll have your friends bring up your breakfast," Izzie said, barely hiding her smile. She turned and closed the door behind her without waiting for a response.

Kai was still in the bed, laughing his cute ass off. I threw a pillow at him before stalking to the bathroom. A few minutes later, he joined me in the tub and we took turns cleaning each other. When we were done, he helped me oil and brush my hair before heading for the door. At some point, Izzie had come back and brought him some clothes, so he was now dressed in his long-sleeved black tunic. It had silver embroidery, a nod to the goddess Luna and her forever silver hair. It was paired with black pants and black boots. Izzie hadn't been able to bring his weapons, but even without them, he looked every bit a captain.

"Maven, no." Alek's warm voice came through the door just as it was thrown open.

"We waited long enough out here. Our best friend is going on trial for her life; the least Kai could do is give us some time with her." Maven burst through the door, dreads billowing behind her, dressed in a lavender t-shirt and skinny blue jeans that accented her body in all the right spots.

She shoved past Kai and gathered me in her arms. "Yo, I have missed you so much. Alek has been insufferable this whole time. It didn't take long to gather everyone, and we had to go back to the bar and of course, he kept fawning over the bartender."

"I missed you too, Maven," I said, pulling away from her with a laugh.

"Sariyah don't believe her; we could have met everyone here, but she insisted on the bar so she could go stand in a corner and brood with Remy." Aleksander walked in, holding a tray with bagels, muffins, and various jams. He set it on the table and embraced me as well.

"Welp," Kai said, "now that my replacements are here, I'm going to go...well anywhere but here." He grabbed a bagel and fist-bumped Alek on the way out. Maven stuck her tongue at him and he returned the gesture with an obscene one of his own.

He blew me a kiss and was on his way.

"So, from the glowing look on your face and those rumpled sheets, I think it's safe to say my boy had a good explanation for everything," Alek said, wagging his eyebrows suggestively.

"Yes, he did," I retorted. "He explained again and again and again," I said just as suggestively. He and Maven made faces and pretended to gag and vomit, but I know they were happy for me.

"So, what now?" Maven asked. We had moved to the sitting room beyond the bedroom and dove into breakfast. Maven picked around at her second muffin while Alek and I sipped coffee. Mine filled with sugar and heavy cream and his black as midnight. We had spent most of the early hours talking about what they had done the last three days and who all agreed to come to speak on my behalf. Apparently, King Charles was already on his way after being alerted by the council. He had arrived the following day with Josephine by his side. Jezlyn, Ellie, and Amethyst had come with them today and Remy was meeting up later. Either to celebrate my freedom or to court Mave, only time would tell. Apparently, they had really hit it off. Alek said they were practically inseparable.

"Well, now we wait. I can't leave this room and my powers are pretty much cut off."

"That explains it," Alek said. "I couldn't put my finger on it, but when we walked in, something felt off. He reached out to a candle on the foyer and tried to light it with magic. "Even though elemental magic isn't a strong point of mine, I should have been able to do that."

"Well, we are going to stay here until the very end. After all, you're the reason we are here."

We spent the last few hours cracking jokes and telling stories. We tried as hard as we could to not look at the time. I teased Maven about her romance with Remy and she made fun of me for being so quick to take Kai back to bed. It felt like old times. We had just turned our attention to Alek to interrogate him about Bella when Izzie's familiar knock floated through the room."

"Damn, is it time already?" I said. Suddenly my body felt like stone. I could potentially be walking to my death. If the Council heard everything we had to say and just didn't care, they would sentence me right there. I willed myself to be strong. I didn't come this far to give up now.

"Come in Izzie," I yelled. "I'm ready. Let's get this day over with."

"Just so you know Sai," Maven said, "I and Alek already talked and if there is anything other than a not-guilty verdict, we plan on snatching you and running." She smiled wickedly.

"This time, I don't think we would have to worry about Kai chasing us either," Alek added with a laugh.

Izzie wasn't alone when she came into the sitting room. Besides her were two guards I hadn't met yet. In one's hands were the spelled cuffs. I slowly got up and raised my hands out so he could put them on.

"I'm sorry Princess," he said, "it's just protocol."

"It's ok; I know you're just doing your duty."

He and the other guard exchanged a glance before continuing.

"Just so you know, Captain Gerard has been nothing but nice to us. Before he came along, we were stuck with grunt work and not taken seriously. Now we have real duties and are able to march alongside the other warriors." His voice started to tremble, and the other guard touched his shoulder. More confidently, he said, "We are loyal to the crown, of course, but we are also Loyal to Captain Kai. So, if the time comes, we will heed his orders." They both looked at me sternly. The rest didn't need to be said aloud. If Kai gave the order to protect me, they would do without question.

The walk down to the courtyard seemed like it took ages. In reality, it was only a few minutes. The Council had set up a table directly in the middle, with one smaller table across from it. There was no need to have a prosecutor as they would be my judge, jury, and if need be, my executioner.

I sat across from them and looked them directly in the eye one by one. Each one met me back with a look of resolve, with the exception of Marcel. He looked too damn happy to be here.

On either side of the table, flanking Marcel and Regina, were two guards. Behind them were three more guards, Kai being directly in the middle. I had never seen him look so serious. Even in practice combat, he was always goofy but stern. The look on his face now as he stood guard was truly horrifying. He looked as cold and stone-faced as the other guards and would not make eye contact with me. I knew in my heart he had to play the role but it still stung just a bit.

In the distance a bell tolled 12 times, signaling the afternoon and the beginning of my trial.

"Sariyah Marie Devereaux, please rise," King Charles bellowed.

I shakily stood up from my seat.

"You are being charged with the murder of the Queen Regent Charlotte Anne Devereaux. How do you plead."

"Not guilty," I said. "I am here today not only to prove my innocence, but I believe I can also provide enough proof as to who really killed my Aunt."

"You may begin."

And so I stood there in front of the council, the people I loved, and the people I was supposed to rule, and I told my story. I told them as much as I could without incriminating Kai and thankfully, they didn't ask too much about the marigold or Alek's Mind Walking. King Charles managed to steer them away from delving too much into those specifics. As I recanted my tale, they would call upon each witness to explain their role. Alek even went as far as to talk about his father – who was noticeably absent – and his involvement. One by one, my friends, old and new stepped up to defend me. When it came to King Charles, he had Josephine tell both his part and hers. It took hours and by the end of it, I knew for sure they believed what happened. I just wasn't sure they cared.

"That was quite a tale you have spun Miss Devereaux," Marcel sneered, not even trying to hide his contempt. Behind him, his son's eyes flashed momentarily with anger and his hand gripped his sword just a little tighter. Marcel continued, not knowing one wrong move and he would be the one executed today.

"There seems to be one key thing missing and that's your parents. I mean, if they are truly alive as you say...well where are they?"

"I have no idea. But if I am granted my freedom, I will spend every moment I have finding them and bringing them to justice."

"The same justice as your aunt?" Regina asked. "If your father really committed these crimes, as you say, not only did she fail to bring him to justice, but she also lied and covered for him. As his daughter, who's to say you won't do the same?"

It was a fair question.

"My father died when I was nine years old, Councilwoman Regina." I turned my head to look at her directly. "The man I knew, the man I loved, he walked out of my life and has been gone ever since. He and my mother committed atrocities not only against our country, not only against our people, had he been given a chance, I no doubt believe he would have killed me too. As for my mother, well, Queen Charlotte raised me for the majority of my life. When she died, my mother did too. I am not as soft-hearted as she was. When the time comes for Kalen Devereaux to die, it will be by my sword."

I found more conviction in my voice as I spoke. I could hear the crowd cheering behind me. I was no longer speaking like the little princess they had known before; I was speaking as their Queen. The rightful heir to the throne. After hearing everything Charlotte had done for her people to keep them safe, there was no doubt they loved her even more. As her successor, the one she had protected the most, a lot of that love and respect trickled down to me.

I couldn't tell if the Council had been moved by my words or the crown's support. All of their faces were stony and reserved.

"Now that we have heard from all of the witnesses, we shall adjourn to deliberate."

They stood up one by one and returned to the castle where they would decide my fate. I hoped like hell they would make the right choice.

Several hours passed and the sun began to sink. It seemed like a decision would not be made today. I wasn't sure whether to be relieved or more scared. Kai and several of the guards had gone into the castle with them and had yet to return. The two who had brought me out here stood sentient by my side. Some of the people in the crowd came up to wish me luck or tell me how brave I was before heading back to their homes. They had kids to get ready or jobs early the next day and either way, they would be told of the verdict. After they were gone, there was no talking, no movement, just waiting and more waiting.

I had my head rested in my palms, the cuffs making it difficult to get comfortable. I was about to close my eyes out of sheer boredom rather than fatigue when the whispering began. The Guards came out of the castle, Kai leading them. Sandwiched between them were Councilwomen Regina and Freya. King Charles followed behind, his face tired and worn. He had deep wrinkles in his forehead like he'd spent the last few hours with a furrowed brow.

Marcel Gerard was nowhere to be seen and I took that as a good sign. He would not have wanted to hear them declare me innocent and take away his chance to remove me from his son's life.

I held my breath as they gathered around the table.

"Sariyah, please stand," Freya, paper in hand, began to speak.

"We were here to determine whether or not you were responsible for Queen Regent Charlotte's death. You detailed many things we were unaware of due to your aunt withholding knowledge and even passing judgment down without conferring with the council. You abandoned your duties as princess and fled the capital as well as dragging two of our best warriors with you."

They missed the part where they came along willingly, I said in my head, too afraid of what was coming to speak up.

"Those transgressions cannot be forgiven. However, Queen Charlotte paid for hers with her life. Some members of the Council felt it was only fair for you to pay with yours as well."

My stomach fell like a stone in a pit. I really couldn't believe this. After all the witness testimonies, they would kill me just because I ran?

The crowd behind me began to shout. They were just as shocked and angry as I was. Maven and Alek tried to rush to my side, but the guards around me prevented them. At Kai's beckoning, the crowd began to quiet down so that Freya could finish. I couldn't bear to look at his face. I was afraid to see the pain and hurt that would mirror my own. Instead, I kept my head down and waited for my sentence to be passed.

"Indeed, there were members who felt this way," she continued, "however, that was not a unanimous sentiment.

"There were those of us who were moved by your bravery and your resolve. Especially after learning from the captain sent to dispatch you that you came here of your own volition." My head snapped up to look at Kai. His face was still unreadable, but he had protected me once again. My savior until the end.

"So, with that being said, while we cannot agree that your father Kalen Devereaux and your mother Queen Sofia Devereaux were alive or responsible for your Aunt Charlotte's death, we do believe that you are innocent. Your punishment for your desertion will be decided at another time. Guards, please remove the cuffs."

The crowd behind me erupted in cheers. Maven and Alek broke through the guards to rush me and embrace me, their faces wet with tears.

The joy was short-lived, though.

A figure came clapping very loudly and sarcastically out of the crowd.

"Well, well, well, this was not exactly how I thought things would go."

At the sound of that voice, my blood ran cold. I didn't have to turn around to know to whom it belonged. After 14 years of not hearing it, I would still know that voice from anywhere.

It belonged to my dad. Kalen Devereaux.
The King had returned.

"My dear Sariyah, my how you have grown. I almost didn't recognize you. Turn around dear, let your old man take a good look at you."

I was frozen to the spot. Kai, Maven, and Aleksander had moved to my side, creating a semi-circle around me. Even with this nest of safety, I couldn't move my feet to face him. I knew that once I did, it would be over. Any hope I had of keeping the good memories of my dad would be gone and would be replaced by this monster when I looked into his eyes.

"Sweetheart, don't tell me you're afraid?" He must have moved towards me because I felt Kai press against my back and I heard him unsheathe his sword.

"Don't you come any further," he growled. "I won't let you touch her."

"Little boy, I have been fighting since before you were born," Kalen growled back. "If you think a sword will keep me at bay, you are in for a surprise. Those weapons you guards keep are all for show. I could shift right now and tear you all apart, daughter included."

"You take one more step towards her and you won't have the opportunity to shift." Maven, a weapon all on her own with an axe to grind, took a step forward. "Besides, I don't think it's fair for Kai to kill you. I owe you one for my mother."

"Ah, you're the Taro girl I presume. You look just like your mother. Even more so in a minute when I kill you. You'll definitely look like twins then."

That was all it took to set Maven off. I felt her rush forward and I could do nothing to stop her. My stupid feet wouldn't move. All I could do was stand there and listen to the grunts and thuds as my best friend attacked my father.

"Wow, the warrior training has not been lost on you, vampire. You could possibly give me a run for my money. Too bad your mother wasn't as gifted."

The clashing continued as Maven went in for another blow. Kalen artfully dodged her while antagonizing her about her mother's death.

"It's a shame dear, that your mother didn't put up this much of a fight. I'm almost sad I didn't get the final blow."

"What the hell are you talking about," she screamed. "I saw you. I saw you kill my mom and I heard you laugh."

"If you were truly there dear then you would have known I didn't come alone. I have no reason to lie. Yes, I was there to kill your mother for ratting us out and helping those wretched kids escape. But it wasn't me who gutted her like the pig she was."

"Alek," I whisper. "Get these cuffs off me," I said sternly. I had had enough. I had heard enough.

Alek's eyes darted from me to Mave. She was bleeding from her mouth but was otherwise unharmed. My father was across from her. Other than his shirt being a little disheveled, he was fine as well.

Neither one of them looked at me, too focused on each other. They circled each other like wolves.

I did feel a set of eyes on me. I searched the crowd for who it could be. Most of the people had fled when my dad came out. The few who dared hadn't taken their eyes off him and Maven.

About halfway through, I found them. It wasn't just one set of eyes, it was two. One set purple and the other set green. The latter belonged to my mother. She didn't look particularly happy, and the sentiment was definitely returned. I had no idea who the other woman was, although if I had to guess, it was the shifter who helped my father escape.

"Damnit," Maven shouted, tearing me away from my mother's watchful eyes. My father had lunged at her, slashing her chest with his claws. His eyes gleamed as he watched the blood flow down her body and stain the ground. It wasn't fatal, but it was enough to slow her down.

"Alek please, you have to get these cuffs off so I can help Maven."

"Sariyah, I don't know if I can. This is ancient magic. These runes go back to the age of the goddesses. That's not something I'm familiar with."

"Please try; Maven is going to get seriously hurt if I don't help her and I am useless with these cuffs on."

"Is that so?"

Oh shit. I spoke too loudly. My father's attention was now on me and the cuffs I held out to Aleksander.

"Here I was thinking you were frozen in fear, and this whole time you didn't even have your abilities. That must be some magic too, if the witch can't break it. Stronger than the binds I had to put on your power."

"What are you talking about," I asked. "I have been able to shift since before you died. Nothing has changed."

He tsked. "That isn't true at all. See, I loved you. I didn't want you to be more powerful than me, but I also didn't want to kill you. Your mother thought otherwise. The first time you shifted was normal at first, a cute little pup. You would run and chase your tail; it was adorable. Your mother," he nodded his head to Sofia, "was ecstatic that you were a little wolf just like her. After a while though, you got bigger and faster. And soon, you could even outrun your mom and me. Then the other kids began showing powers. We had finally begun to believe that the prophecy may be true."

"And that's when you started murdering them?" I yelled indignantly. I don't know what his point was with this walk down memory lane, but we all know how it ended.

"You went around murdering small children all just so you wouldn't lose your power! All to keep the goddesses from walking the Earth again because you didn't want anyone to be worshipped over you."

"Partly correct. We still didn't fully believe the prophecy. Just because there were some strong kids doesn't mean any of them could beat me. Besides, none of them had the eyes the Oracle spoke of," he said. His focus was now wholly on me. Maven was on the ground behind him, her wound now a slow trickle. She looked at me with pleading eyes, silently begging me not to get involved.

I couldn't just sit here and let my father beat on her. I had to do something.

"So what was it then. What was the reason you started killing the kids?"

"You were, darling. You and those awful eyes."

"My awful eyes?" I said in bewilderment. What was wrong with my eyes?

On your ninth birthday, we went for a run like we always did. With the bindings in place, you grew at a normal pace. However, you were so excited about your new little friends and starting warrior training. Apparently, such strong emotions caused a break in the bindings. When we came back from our run, one of your eyes had turned red.

"At first, we had thought maybe you had burst a blood vessel, but when you blinked, it was gone. That's when I knew I had to kill you."

He said it so matter of fact, so nonchalantly. My father. My flesh and blood dad was going to kill me.

"Don't look so surprised sweetie; there could be no exceptions." He turned back to Maven and kicked her square in the chest. Her body flew back and slammed into a tree. I could hear the sickening crunch of her bones as they made contact. Her body slumped to the ground, she wasn't unconscious, but she definitely would not be able to move for a while. Both Kai and Alek tensed.

They took one look at each other and then they both attacked my father.

"What the hell!" I screamed. How could they be so reckless? They watched what he did to Maven.

As they ran to Maven's aid, Kai tossed his sword to Alek and unleashed his deadly set of claws. Landing on opposite sides of my father, they attacked him from every angle. It was like watching a dance. Kai would strike high and Alek would strike low, the sword just barely missing my father's legs.

His grin grew wider and wider as he dodged all of their attacks. It was like a cat playing with two mice. At least Kai and Alek were able to keep up with him and dodge his attacks as well. The two of them together were a formidable team.

It looked like they might be enough to overpower my father when he landed a blow. Alek, who had just been about to swing the sword and give Kai an opening to strike, was suddenly blown black.

I screamed as I heard my father's fist connect with his skull. My father had been holding back all along, playing around to get a feel for their movements. When the time was right, he struck hard and fast. Alek had no time to react.

Kai, however, was in a whole different league. My father turned to strike, but he fainted left and instead dealt a blow of his own right to my father's ribs. Stumbling back, he seemed in shock at the power Kai exhibited.

"So," he said tensely, "you were holding back as well. Well, now that the lightweights are out of the way, let me see what you got, little Marcel."

"I am nothing like my father," he spat. "I'll let loose if you do though. Let's see the full power of the demon king."

Snarling, my father threw a claw at Kai, who ducked just in time. Now that they both had let go, they were moving even faster; trading blows one after another, neither quick enough to land one.

Seeing Maven and Alek on the ground bleeding at my father's hands angered me. Watching Kai have to defend all of us angered me even more. I wasted precious moments being too scared to turn around and now my friends were left unprotected. I could feel my wolf bristling just under my skin, yearning to get into this fight. I thought about what my father had said. The last time I broke through the binds, it had been because I displayed extreme emotion. If I could do it again, maybe it would be enough to release me from the cuffs.

Kai was starting to slow down. Even after being imprisoned for 14 years, my father hadn't lost his touch. Stories had been told of his fights and how he'd clawed his way up to become alpha of the shifters. Not many people would go toe to toe with him and even less would survive.

I had to do something though. I tried to think of all the happy moments I had with my friends, with Kai and my aunt. I tried to focus all those feelings into the cuffs as I flexed my wrists, trying to will them to break. It was no use though; nothing was powerful enough.

"Sariyah move!"

My father had enough of toying with Kai, and somewhere in the fight, he had picked up the sword Alek dropped when he was hit and tossed it fiercely in my direction.

Maven had yelled to warn me, but it was too late. I closed my eyes and readied myself for the hit. But it never came.

When I opened my eyes, Kai was standing in front of me. He was smiling, but blood was leaking from the corner of his mouth.

I looked down and saw the cause. The sword that was meant for me was sticking directly through his chest.

Out in the Open

I couldn't hear anything but screaming. Whether it was mine or my friends' I do not know. One moment Kai was fighting my dad; the next, he was taking a death blow meant for me.

My heart had finally and completely broken. I don't know exactly what happened next. There was an Earth-shattering roar and then everything was red. I could feel my wolf bursting forward. I could feel my bones shifting, breaking, and reattaching, but it felt different this time. I focused all of my hurt and anger on my change. I pictured myself ripping my father's head off his shoulders. My wolf responded in kind. My nails elongated and turned to claws. My clothes tore as my fur came bursting through. My fangs burst through my gums several inches longer than they had been before. This shift was unlike anything else I had experienced. This must have been what my father was afraid of. This was the wolf he had bound for years.

The people in the remaining crowd had begun to scatter. In this form, I could rip this whole courtyard apart. And if it meant killing Kalen – I would never call him father again – then I sure as hell would.

"There it is," he whispered. "There's the beast I should have killed." His face was a mixture of anger and wonder, but not fear. Even as I am, he still thought he could beat me. He was as delusional as he was evil.

I couldn't speak as a wolf. I didn't need to though. Soon enough, he would know exactly what I felt. He would feel the pain that was coursing through my veins and fueling the strength I have. I could only smell the faint scent of Kai's blood lingering. Someone must have taken his body away.

Good, I thought, I don't want his body to be torn apart. He deserved a proper burial.

I padded around on all fours, keeping my eyes on Kalen. This body was much sturdier, and I needed to get a grip on it and fast.

Kalen still had his claws out, but other than that, his panther stayed just below the surface of his skin. I could sense him wanting to change but not sure if it was necessary just yet.

I exploded forward, no warning. One moment I was staring at him, picturing me ripping through his chest and the next moment, I was airborne. This wolf was much more sensitive now that she was free. I moved more on reflex and instinct rather than an actual strategy. I landed in the spot where Kalen had just been. He was still pretty quick and was able to move at the very last moment. I wasn't letting up though. I charged and he dodged. The smile that he wore when facing my friends had now turned into a grimace. As strong as he was, I was stronger. As fast as he was, I was faster.

He was moving out of the way, but I wasn't giving him a chance to go on the offensive. From the corner of my eyes, I saw Sofia lurking. She was mid-shift and I took my attention from Kalen just long enough to emit another loud roar. Her being a werewolf as well, she was able to hear the meaning in my growls.

"Stay," I said. "You'll have your turn to die next." I was not having it today. Because of these two incredibly selfish people, I lost so many things that were important to me. I don't care what the cost was to me. I was getting my revenge

I was all rage and power. Sofia had no choice but to heel. She was no longer the Alpha here and if she stepped in, I would have no choice but to show her.

The momentary flex of my power cost me.

Seeing an opportunity in the distraction, Kalen struck me right in my side. He sent me tumbling, but I was agile enough to land on my feet.

Shit, he may have broken a rib here. I had to keep my focus on him. Sofia wouldn't dare intrude now. If she lost to me out here in the open, she would cement my status as Alpha. Not that it mattered to me. I had no desire to take the throne. I could only hope to survive long enough to defeat them. And then I would join Kai.

"You should never take your eyes off your opponent Sariyah Devereaux. Did your aunt not teach you that?

"Well, let me teach you something else." He started to move towards me, but my focus was solely on him now. I watched his body language and prepared to rip off whatever limb he decided to throw next.

I felt it before I could even sense it. Something large and strong landed on my back and sunk its teeth into my neck at the same moment Kalen attacked. I couldn't shake this new creature off in time to block his blow, so it hit me with full force.

The creature rolled with me after I sustained the punch, not letting go of the chunk of neck it held in its mouth. The canines were as long as a wolf's, so I know it was not Sofia.

For fuck's sake. I had totally forgotten the other shifter that was here. She must have been hiding somewhere out of sight, waiting to jump me.

We thrashed around violently, trying to keep out of the way of Kalen and get the bitch off my damn neck.

Thank the Goddesses, Sofia hadn't regained her confidence and joined in. I would not have been able to evade Kalen with all three of them attacking.

"Keep your head on a swivel; that's today's lesson," Kalen jeered as he threw a series of punches and kicks. "Enemies can be all around."

This girl still had a strong hold on my neck and I was losing a lot of blood. My speed was starting to slow down, and I needed to get her off me quickly so I could start to heal.

The opportunity came just as Kalen was about to throw another punch. She relaxed her bite just enough for me to swing her around and the punch hit her directly in her spine. The force of hit caused her jaws to release.

She whimpered and scurried away.

Finally, the wounds on my neck began to heal immediately. I regained some of my strength and hoped it was enough to finish this.

Kalen was pissed. His eyes full of rage as he looked at the crumpled body of his partner. He hadn't had enough time to pull his punch and the force definitely broke something, if not severing her spine completely.

"Useless," he spat. "Utterly goddamn useless. Enough playing around. I've indulged you enough Sariyah."

As he spoke, his body began to take his panther form. For the first time since we had begun fighting, Kalen was bothered enough to actually shift.

Which meant I was probably fucked.

Sure enough, as soon as his beast was freed, he lunged right for my throat. I rolled right and was able to barely move out the way, his canines scraping so close to me I could almost feel them.

Shifted, we were at our most powerful, and Kalen had been holding back for far too long. He now had me on the defensive. It was hard to believe this was the man that once rocked me in his arms to sleep.

When I say he had been holding back, he'd really been holding back. He came at me fast, but I was faster. We were a myriad of bites and slashes rolling around on the courtyard stone. We traded hit for hit, our fur sticky with blood. Neither of us was willing to back down. I guess that's where I got my determination.

At least he is quieter; I thought while dodging his next flurry of swipes. Without his incessant teasing and commentary, I could really let go and allow the wolf to take over. My senses were more acute, but I was still moving slower because of the damage I had sustained. Every time Kalen leaped, I moved out of the way like a seriously violent game of tag. Every now and then, he would get a nip in or his claws would catch my face or my shoulder. Even slowed down, I could still see him anticipate his movements. Taking his advice, I kept my distance from him and also kept Sofia and the strange woman who also was a panther apparently in my field of vision. They would not get the drop on me so easily again.

I could feel Kalen getting agitated; his fur was standing up on his back. He wanted this to end just as much as I did. Unfortunately, with all the evading I had done, he could still back me in. I was pressed into the giant statue of the goddesses in the middle of the courtyard. Even though Sofia had not entered the fray, she was still on my left, looking a little pissed. The other woman had recovered enough to shift back to human and was now on my right.

Shit shit shit. I couldn't see a way out. I could rush Kalen, but I would run the risk of one or both of these women attacking me as well. Sofia looked pissed enough not to care about losing her alpha status.

My body was healing quickly, but there were too many injuries sustained. I wasn't able to regain enough strength to hold them off, and for what or who would be coming to help me. Maven was hurt, Alek was hurt, and Kai, Kai was dead. The anger I had felt at that moment returned to me. I didn't care anymore. No matter what happened next, I wouldn't let them go unscathed. I crouched low on my hindlegs and prepared myself to attack. Kalen did the same. Not wanting to wait to see what I was going to do, he came rushing through the air. I met him mid-leap and bit down as hard as I could. My teeth sunk into his arm the same time two sets of jaws sunk into my hindlegs.

We all crashed into the hard ground around us. I had no more strength left. Against my will, I shifted back. Kalen must have been drained from the fight as well as he stood over me in his human form. Somehow his pants managed to stay intact, and for that, I was grateful. I would hate for the last image I see in this life to be my naked father.

"You put up a good fight," he said, kicking my already broken body. "Had you actually had training in that body, you might have bested me today. My final lesson to you dear Sariyah, is this: Experience beats brawn every day," as he spoke, he raised Kai's sword. The same one he had used to impale him.

"Consider this justice coming full circle. You'll get to die by the same sword as the man you loved. How poetic."

His evil smile returned as he swung the sword in a near-perfect arch. I could hear it sing as it cut through the wind. I closed my eyes and braced myself for the impact, but it never came.

Kalen had drawn the sword down, but he was frozen in his tracks. A portal had opened up directly to his side and through it came an astonishingly beautiful woman. She was 5'8" and decked in all-black battle armor, hair tied up in a tight bun. She had raven-colored hair and eyes as green and deep as emeralds. The queen's emblem was emblazoned across her chest plate.

She looked like a Goddess and a Warrior. Kalen must have hit me harder than I had thought because that could be the only reason for the woman standing before me.

My aunt was supposed to be dead. And she had never looked this badass.

"Stay down Sai," she said without looking at me. "It's my turn."

Queen Vs Queen

"I killed you. I saw you dead. There's no way." Finally, the smirk that had haunted us throughout this battle was wiped off his face.

"No brother, you saw only what I wanted you to see. Only what I needed you to see. If you had even thought for a moment I was walking this earth; you would have never come out of your hole."

"No, it's not possible," he sputtered, starting to back up. "I killed you!" he roared.

"You were always short-sighted, brother. You only cared about power and it blinded you. You were always concerned about instant gratification and it never crossed your mind that your actions would have consequences. You truly thought you could walk this world unchecked and that is why you didn't see this coming, and it's also why you will lose."

Kalen had used up whatever strength he had left for that final attack. He was at Charlotte's mercy. If she even deigned to show him any.

She drew two Karambit daggers from her waist, each one curved and sharp. The runes in the designs glowed as she held them. She must have had them spelled by a strong witch, making them that much more deadly. Spinning them in her hands, she began to stalk Kalen, who was quickly drawing back.

"How did you survive," he hissed. "I punched a hole straight through you. There was no way you could have healed fast enough to live."

"And yet here I am." Charlotte was fast. She hit Kalen with a series of blows in succession, cutting his face and chest with her daggers. The blood splattered everywhere. Kalen swiped at her wildly, but she jumped back and he missed her completely.

Even as injured as he was, his blood should not have continued spilling as quickly as it was. Instead, everywhere the daggers sliced, the blood was just pouring.

"What are you doing to me," Kalen screamed, realizing it at the same time I did. None of the wounds Charlotte had given him were healing.

"Well, you made a lot of enemies in your short reign as King dear brother. One of them being the witches. That oracle you cast out, as sweet as she may be, definitely held a grudge. The first time we fought, she gave me these, and I was too soft-hearted to use them. She spelled them to slow down our fast healing enough to be able to kill you."

Way to go, Josephine! I cheered silently. I had to remember to thank her and take her for a drink.

"No," he gasped. That was all Kalen was able to utter. He tried to run for it, but he couldn't get far in his state. Charlotte was on him in seconds, dragging him back each time.

"Where are you going brother? It's such a nice day for a family reunion. I mean, why should you and Sofia be the only ones allowed to return from the dead?"

She tossed him by his neck into the courtyard once again.

This time he stayed down. He glared at her and then to me and then back to her.

"I hate you both," was all he managed to muster.

"I think that's enough Charlotte. It isn't fair to face your brother when he has been through not one, not two, but three fights already."

Queen Sofia had finally spoken. As she spoke, she walked up to where Kalen lay. His wounds were still gushing and he was now in a puddle of his own blood. Good. Hopefully, he would die right here and save us the trouble.

Sofia knelt down and examined Kalen. "You there, Mistress," she called to the shifter who had been with them. "Come get my husband while I take care of this imposter Queen."

The shifter didn't move at first. She had locked eyes with Charlotte, who was all but taunting her to move. The second she moved to join us in the courtyard, Charlotte was on her, daggers at her throat.

"You didn't think I would just let you take my brother, did you?" she laughed wickedly. I had never heard her so cold and savage. This was a different person than the woman who raised me. I had heard stories of her prowess as a warrior, but to me, she was always just goofy and funny. Until she became Queen, and then she was cool and aloof.

My wounds were starting to catch up to the healing finally. I was still going to need to see a medic, but I was able to push myself up so that I was in a sitting position

"Ouch," I winced. Apparently, there was more than one broken rib. I surveyed the scene before me. At the edge of the courtyard, my supposed-to-be-dead aunt stood face to face, daggers out, with the woman my mother referred to as "Mistress." A little tidbit I put away in my memory for later.

Kalen lay several feet away, still bleeding pretty badly, and my mom knelt beside him, glaring at the back of Charlotte's head.

How did we get here? If I weren't actually living this, I wouldn't have believed it myself.

"Come on Charlotte, let the wench go. Face me. After all, it's my crown you took and my daughter you poisoned."

I snapped my head to Sofia so quickly I think I may have broken a vertebra.

"How the hell did she poison me when you and Kalen tried to kill me?" I said hoarsely.

If she heard me, she didn't act like it. She didn't even turn her head to look in my direction.

I continued anyways. "Aunt Charlotte raised me. She took care of me when you died. She was more of a mother to me than you ever were." That last remark may have been a little too far.

My mother stood up slowly, looked me in my face, and threw a dagger at my head.

It missed.

"Sariyah, are you ok?" Charlotte yelled.

"Don't you ever disrespect me again," Sofia snarled. "I may have gone along with your father's plan, and hell, I may have even agreed with parts of it. But I never wanted to kill you. It wasn't your father's idea to bind your powers. It was mine."

"That's a lie; I heard him say it was his idea. We all heard him."

"Your father, for all his wit and charm, was always a cunning liar. He was antagonizing you. Isn't that right dear?" she nudged him with her foot and he let out a painful groan.

"He wants to be the leader but never wants to take the blame."

"Then why did you stay by his side?" I asked.

"Because he was my husband and the King. I fought way too hard to be anything less than a Queen, even if that means I have to deal with mistresses." The glare she gave the woman did not go unnoticed.

It was like one bomb dropping after the other. I could hardly keep up.

"You still murdered children," I said. "Even if you saved me, you still sat back and allowed so many children to die."

"I don't have to explain anything to you," she said back. "You may have grown up, but you're still a child. Should you ever wear the crown, you'll see, sometimes you have to make the hard decisions."

With that she turned back to Charlotte. "Let her go and face me Char. Let's duel for old time's sake. Besides, I owe you one for trapping me."

"If you don't, I'll rip Sariyah's throat out myself."

She didn't move towards me. She didn't have to. The threat hanging in the air was enough.

Mother of the year, telling me she wanted to save me and then threatened to kill me the next.

I could see Charlotte's back tense up. She was probably determining whether or not to call Sofia's bluff. Slowly she lowered her arms, daggers still out, and stepped aside.

Mistress wasted no time. She raced to Kalen, scooped him up, and fled into the forest.

My aunt and mother faced each other. Charlotte with daggers and Sofia with Kai's blade. They circled each other, each waiting for the other to make a move. The only sound was their boots scraping the ground and my labored breathing.

They both paused at the same time and looked at the castle behind me.

Someone was approaching. The footsteps slowed down as they got closer to what was now our battlefield.

"Hurry and take her, vampire," Sofia said and nodded her head at me. "See to it that she gets patched up. She is going to need her strength for what's to come."

What the hell is with this woman. How can she act so motherly one minute and then crazy the next? The two versions of her were already clashing in my head, which was not helping.

"It's ok Maven. She won't attack," Sofia scoffed and rolled her eyes, bouncing Kai's blade in her hand.

The next second, Maven's hands wrapped around my shoulders as she gingerly but swiftly tossed me on her back.

Here vampire," Sofia shouted as Maven was about to run. I was too exhausted to fight anymore, although I wanted to stay and see who won. My body was worn out, bloody and beaten. Being here, I would only be in the way.

Sofia tossed Maven Kai's sword and she caught it with the hand that wasn't holding me up.

"He was a brave fighter. He would have made a good king." I couldn't see her face, but I could almost picture genuine sadness from her tone.

"Now get my daughter the hell out of here, vampire."

And just like that, the nurturing mother was gone again, replaced by the Murdering Queen.

Maven wasted no time getting us the hell out of there. Finally able to rest, my mind finally gave in. As I slipped once again into that darkness, I could faintly here the sound of metal hitting metal.

This is how it was going to end.

Queen vs. Queen

Death in the Family

I came to, in the infirmary four days ago; Maven had told me what happened. I was so distraught she had to hold me down to keep me from feeling.

"Sariyah, I am so sorry; I know how much you loved her. I know you are hurting, but you're still not fully healed."

"The council has already decided they will not bury her until you are well."

I didn't care what the council wanted. Hell I didn't even care that I was still badly hurt. I needed to see her. I needed to look into her face and see that she was gone.

"Maven, I need to say goodbye," I said, choking on my tears. "I need to tell her goodbye. I never got to say goodbye." I kept trying to get out of bed. I kept thrashing around and throwing things.

Eventually, they had to sedate me just to keep me quiet.

That is how I spent the next few days. Drugged and going in and out of sleep as my body healed from the horrendous amount of trauma it had endured. I had several broken ribs, a fractured sternum, fractured collar bone, three broken fingers, and a bruised lower back—all courtesy of dear old dad.

Every chance I had, I would ask to go see her and every time, they would say, "Maybe tomorrow."

I started to lash out at them as well. Why were they keeping me from her? They said they understood but could they really? Maven and Alek took turns babysitting me, making sure I didn't leave and when they couldn't, they had the Guards watch me instead. When I was finally cleared to leave the infirmary, I was rushed to the mortuary where they had been holding her. I had to see her for myself. Really see that she was dead. I broke down right there beside her now cold body. I screamed, wailed, and hit the walls with so much force that my knuckles were bloody and raw. The guards called for Maven and she came, but she also stayed outside and allowed me to grieve.

I had just gotten her back only to lose her again. I'm not sure what I thought the outcome was supposed to be. I just assumed that somehow they would both survive. I cried until my throat was sore and my eyes were red and puffy. I wound up falling asleep in there and Maven had to carry me to bed.

I wouldn't go back to the compound. Instead, I opted to keep my room at the castle. That place held too many memories for me and those wounds were nowhere near closing. The next few days went by in a blur. There were arrangements to be made. No one wanted to decide without my input. What flowers should we have, what should she wear, where did I want her buried. I was physically there but not mentally. I merely sat in a chair and pointed. No one tried to push me. Instead, they tiptoed around me as if they were walking on eggshells. Treating me as if I was a fragile piece of china on the edge of a tall table. One wrong move and I would break into a million little pieces. As if I could break any more than I already had. I wanted to tell them how I felt, but I could never find the words. My body may have healed, but I was far from all right. So instead, I just let them manage me with kid gloves and went through the motions day to day. I picked her flowers, picked the menu, I even went over the decorations for the temple. After it was all decided, I went back to my room, curled into my bed and cried.

Today is her funeral. I came to the temple ahead of everyone to have my final moment alone. She looks so beautiful, laying here in her black and gold adorned coffin. She almost looks like she's sleeping. I still couldn't believe this. She is adorned in the finest silk gown. It was silver and white and looked like honey and milk had been swirled together and then poured over her.

They kept her hair down so that her curls would be framing her face, making her look like a princess. She wasn't a princess, though. No, she was far from it.

She was Queen. She was stubborn and fierce but also showed she could be caring and kind. Even though she had made some pretty awful choices in the end, a part of me could no longer hold any anger towards her.

I loved her; beyond all reason, I loved her. Today I would mourn her, and I would bury her.

I knew there would be no point. The sooner she was laid to rest, the sooner the court and the kingdom could heal and begin again.

Besides, my father was still out there lurking, and needed to be dealt with.

I had to settle for a simple gathering. She would be laid to rest in the family plot; then we would have a pyre and burn her favorite flowers as an offering to the Goddesses.

"Sariyah, are you ready," Maven came to the door. She was wearing a ceremonial gown in gold. "They want to start the service, but we understand if you need more time."

"No it's ok; I've said goodbye already. It's time to put her to rest."

I walked away from the altar and took my seat. The music began to play and slowly, people began to file in. It was a larger crowd than I had expected. People really came to be nosey rather than mourn. Maven and Alek took their seats next to me. There were a few warriors for my protection, but they were mostly for show. Now that my powers were unbound, there was no one in this kingdom that could match me in a fight.

As the music continued to play, people came to pay their respect and leave flowers in her coffin. Pretty soon, it would be overrun. I'd like to think she would have loved this. All the attention on her, people adoring her.

Once everyone had come inside and taken their seats, the music stopped.

Upon the altar stood a woman in all black. Her dress was form-fitting but not inappropriate. There were patterns of gold lace applique that accentuated her petite frame while still making her look regal. Her green eyes shone brightly while she began to speak.

"Thank you all for coming," Charlotte said. Her voice relaid more sympathy than she probably actually felt. "Today, we are here to lay to rest Queen Sofia Devereaux."

Charlotte spoke some more kind words and then came and sat next to me. She placed her hand on my knee but didn't speak. She was the only person who didn't try and placate me. At first, she kept her distance, not knowing how I would feel about her killing my mother. I didn't know how I would feel about it either. When I finally saw her, I ran to her and just hugged her and cried. They were not tears of sadness but of joy.

As sad as I was about Sofia's death, I didn't really know her. Not like I knew Aunt Charlotte. All of the evil things aside, I loved my mother, and Charlotte knew that. She let me ugly cry into her chest, ruining the pretty dress she wore. When I finally could speak, I told her I loved her and she said she knew. That was all it took. As the guards began to take my mother's coffin on her final walk through the court and into the cemetery, she took my hand and we took our place behind it. Maven and Alek joined us and we left.

I was the last person to leave her grave. That's where Kai found me. I couldn't cry anymore, so I just stared at her headstone, wishing it said something else. Wishing that the hell I endured was all some horrible dream.

His fingers brushed against mine as he stood silently next to me. His recovery had taken longer than mine, but it didn't stop him from trying to see me. I was relieved he was alive. We hadn't had any conversations about where we stood, but we really didn't have to. I loved him and he loved me and that's all that mattered, for now.

We stood there until the sun went down, not saying anything, not touching, just watching. He knew that all I needed was someone to just be there with me.

"Come on Kai," I said, finally breaking the silence. "We should go inside; Sofia has had enough attention for the day. Besides, now that the funeral is over it's time for the council to announce the news."

When the news broke the following morning, the court was in a frenzy. People had come from all over to witness the beginning of a new story.

In two weeks. I would be crowned Queen.

"Are you sure you want to do this? You don't have to walk me, you know."

Kai stood in front of the mirror in my room, struggling to put on his cufflinks.

"Of course I want to do this," he said with a little frustration.

"Here, let me help."

"It's not every day your girlfriend becomes Queen. I'm not leaving," he said, kissing me on my forehead. I got his cufflinks on and then turned to adjust my own dress.

I'm just glad they are going to let me have one ceremony. Normally shifters and werewolves would have had a separate ceremony. The wolves would name me their alpha and the shifters would name me their queen.

I was tired of the division though, so Charlotte's last act as Queen was to decree both groups merge as one. There would be no more shifter court and no more werewolf court. There would just be Court. The werewolves and shifters would all be at the ceremony and they would bring offerings for both the goddesses and me. There was some fancy ritual done by some witches and then boom! I would be Queen Sariyah Marie Devereaux.

"I saw Maven down there with Remy. Those two seem to have gotten real cozy. Maybe now she'll be a little less mean."

"Maybe," I said, laughing. "But Remy is just as sarcastic as she is, so we may just have to deal with a double dose of it."

"Goddess, no," he groaned. "One Maven is bad enough; we definitely don't need two."

"Are you ready for all this Sai?" his tone was suddenly serious. "A lot comes with being Queen."

"I mean, I have been preparing my whole life for this. You would think I would be ready, but honestly, I am scared shitless."

I begged Charlotte not to abdicate the throne, but she refused.

"Had I said no, we would have had to deal with your father as King, and I wouldn't wish that on anyone."

His eyes darkened at the mention of his father.

"Do you think he is going to come today?" I asked, trying not to press too hard but genuinely curious.

"I highly doubt it," he said. "He flipped his shit when the council outvoted him. They think he may have had ties to your father and no matter what they weren't going to give him an ounce of authority. Hell, with you and Charlotte making us all one, there isn't even a need for him on the council."

"Wow, I didn't know that. How come they didn't tell me, and how the hell did you know?"

"Charlotte told me," He said slowly. "When she officially went to resign, they had to have a whole meeting about it. You know why she stepped down, right?" He shifted his eyes narrowly at me.

"Yes, I know; Charlotte is stepping down on her duties as Queen so that she can hunt down Kalen and finish what she started." She was hellbent on rectifying her mistake.

"And you're ok with it?" he pressed on. "You took your mom's death pretty hard. I'm sure she would listen to you if you had a different view."

"No," I said firmly. "Kalen made his bed. It's full of the bones of innocent people whose only crimes were being born under the wrong moon. Whatever happens between him and Charlotte is the will of the goddesses, and I will not interfere."

As I said it, I really started to believe it. I saw the monster my father was. The mask he wore was completely removed. Any love I may have had for him disappeared when that sword went through Kai's chest.

"Today is about you, Sariyah Devereaux. Let's forget about our fathers and just actually enjoy ourselves."

Kai was right. There was no need to be bothered about tomorrow's problems when today was supposed to be a celebration.

The ceremony went as expected. Marcel did not show up, thank goddess. Bella did come and she looked beautiful on Aleksander's arm. She had come days after the battle and has not left his side since. I didn't think I would ever see him stop his playboy ways. Maybe it just took the right woman. Maven was in a corner with Remy whispering furiously and laughing. No doubt they were making fun of one of the guests. As if she felt my gaze, she looked up and gave a small wave. Remy tipped his glass as well. Kai had left to grab me a drink after spinning me around for hours on the dance floor. You would have thought this ball was for him the way he made his way through the room, introducing me to everyone. It was nice, and I knew that he would make a good king one day. He would have to propose to me again though, I thought with a chuckle.

The happiness was short-lived.

Kai came rushing back with no drinks in his hand and I could already tell something was wrong.

"Sariyah, the Council is here and they are demanding to see you now."

What the hell, couldn't this wait? I literally have only been Queen for less than a day. I rolled my eyes and followed Kai into the room adjacent to the ballroom.

The door closed tightly, the music behind us becoming faint. In the room was Regina Salvatore, Freya, King Charles, Josephine, and my aunt.

"Alrighty y'all, what's the bad news. Has Kalen been found?"

"No Sariyah, he hasn't, and you may want to take a seat." Aunt Charlotte's tone didn't leave any room for arguing.

I sat down in the nearest chair and braced myself for what I knew was going to be a shitstorm.

"Josephine, if you would," my aunt beckoned the Oracle forward.

"I had a vision Sariyah, about your father. Well, about his children really."

"Children? He doesn't have any children but me...." I looked around the room, confused as hell. Kai was the only one who looked even more confused than I.

"The woman he was with," Charlotte said. "The one your mother called Mistress."

"Yeah, I remember her. What about it?"

"She apparently bore two children years after you were born. Sofia really meant it when she called her Mistress."

"So... I have two siblings. That is not as bad as all the other craziness I've endured. So why are y'all looking so anxious?"

The council members and my aunt all shared nervous glances, silently begging someone else to break the news.

It was Josephine who finally spoke.

"The children are twins. One son, one daughter."

"Their names are Max and Mckenna and they are coming for your throne."

Sariyah 's 9th Birthday

"Why is he here, Sariyah?" Maven stood, hands-on hips, glaring at Kai. "Did you really invite him?"

"Aunt Charlotte said he had to come, Maven; his dad is out of town with my dad."

"Fine!" Maven huffed. She had only been here for a few months, but we were already best friends.

Today was my birthday and we were having a small gathering at my parents' house thanks to my aunt.

Like today, for instance. Aunt Charlotte. She threw this whole party together last minute because my parents forgot, and everything was so perfect. Well, except for her making me invite Kai. He was such a brat sometimes. Any time Maven, Alek, and I did anything remotely fun; he would run and tell on us.

"Trust me; I don't want to be here anymore than you do." Kai narrowed his eyes and snorted at Maven, then scratched his ear, looking uncomfortable. His eyes were narrow slits and seething with anger, or maybe it was discomfort. Ever since his mom left, Aunt charlotte had been making us hang out with him. I wanted to feel bad for him, you know, about his mom, but it was difficult when he was always trying to stir trouble. He was so annoying.

"You could always leave, Kai," I said, smirking. He looked at me for a moment before rolling his eyes and skulking away.

"You guys shouldn't be so mean. Be a little nicer to him." Alek, my other best friend, sauntered over to us; he'd obviously overheard the conversation just in time to scold us for being mean to Kai. He was the only one in our group that actually liked Kai and it was infuriating.

"You could leave with him, too," I told him.

"I would, but I was promised cake and ice cream, and that's way is more important than your feelings- Ouch!" He rubbed his head and yelled as Maven swatted him in the head.

"It's Sariyah's birthday; you don't get to be rude."

"Then why are you here? " Alek said, eyes crinkled with laughter as he danced around Maven's next swing.

"Sariyah Marie Devereaux!" I heard my name being called from across the garden and immediately froze. I could hear the anger in my mother's voice, sharp with anger, and knew that

I had pinched a nerve.

"Come here this instant!"

"Ooohh, Sai's in trouble," Alek said in a singsong voice before heading to the food tables.

I turned around to face her. Even though her voice had been stern, her expression was softer, not one of anger.

"Little Miss, did you tell Kai to leave? After your Aunt and I told you to be nice to him?"

"Umm ... well ... no," I stuttered. "No, it wasn't exactly, like that Mom. He said he didn't want to be here so, I told him he didn't have to be." I tried to make my best pouty face. It always worked on dad.

"Kai?" she chuckled. "Is that true?"

He stuck his head out from behind her, where he was hiding, his brown curls falling all around his face.

"Yes, Ma'am, but only because Maven was being mean to me again."

"Hey, wait a minute! This has nothing to do with me." Maven threw her hands up in protest. Not wanting to meet my mother's steely gaze, she began to walk backwards and almost tripped over a large stone on the ground behind her.

"How many times do I have to tell you? You all need to be nice to each other. That includes you, Kai." My mom pulled him around from behind her and placed him next to me.

"Aleksander, you come over here too and stay away from the candy bowl."

Looking like a kid who got caught with his hand in the cookie jar, Alek walked back over with a sheepish grin and lined up beside us.

"I'm sorry, Queen Sofia, all this arguing between the girls and Kai made me hungry." He looked up at her with the same pouty face I had been trying to achieve, only he did it a whole lot better.

"Way to take sides," I mumbled, sending him a death glare too quickly for my mom to notice. He returned it with a wink of his own.

"Listen, while they are setting up for Sariyah's party, you guys should go inside and behave yourselves. If I hear one word about anyone," —her eyes darted between Maven and me— "being mean. I will shut this whole party down and send all of you home." With that, she turned around and began yelling at one of the servants for how they were placing the balloons in the wrong place.

Just like that, all the wind had been snatched from between my sails. I headed inside, turned towards my friends, and beckoned the others to follow. Kai didn't move at first; he just stood there staring at his feet.

"You heard the Queen," I said over my shoulder. "You'd better come too."

Once we got inside, Alek threw himself onto one of the plush couches, and Maven sat on the floor beneath him. Kai went to sulking in a corner of the room, refusing to meet my eyes.

"So, look," I said. "We gotta start getting along."

"I don't know what you're talking about." Maven was picking invisible lint off one of the couch cushions, her eyes downcast. "We get along just fine."

"You know what I mean, Maven." I shoot a look at Kai. "I am sorry for telling you to leave today Kai. That wasn't nice. Okay, Maven, it's your turn." I shifted my eyes, boring into hers, to show her that I really meant it.

"Sorry," Maven mumbled, eyes still focused on the couch.

"Why are you kids inside?" The voice that floated towards us from the kitchen belonged to none other than Aunt Charlotte. Her hair pulled up into a messy bun and a wide smile on her face; she looked every bit an angel.

"Auntie!" I squealed and threw myself into her arms. She swung me around through the air like I was flying. It made me giggle, and I almost felt like I was flying.

When she finally put me down, I was so dizzy I fell right onto my butt. Maven and Alek roared with laughter. I thought I heard Kai chuckle too.

"I'm so glad you're here," I said. "Mom sent us inside because..." Darn, I didn't want to tell her we were being mean to Kai because she doted on him, just as much as she did me.

"She sent us inside so that we wouldn't bother the servants who were setting up." Kai came out of his corner and stood next to my aunt. This was the first time I had ever seen him lie, let alone cover for us. Usually, he would be the first one to run to tattletale on us.

She ruffled his hair with her hand, and I saw a smile creep across his face.

"We really must do something with this," Aunt Charlotte said playfully.

"Well, since you're all inside, let's play a game of hide-and-seek." She knelt down on the floor and whispered conspiratorially, "The winner gets to have a piece of cake before the party."

At the mention of cake, Alek's ears perked up. "You had me at cake, Lady Charlotte."

"Alrighty. Since Sariyah is the birthday girl, she will go first. Count to ten, and we will all hide, then you have ten minutes to find us. Whomever isn't caught when the time is up is the winner." She paused.

"And one more thing. No magic or magic abilities can be used."

"That's not fair." Maven put her hands on her hips and sighed. "It's not my fault the goddesses blessed me with speed."

"No, it is not," Aunt Charlotte agreed, her emerald eyes sparkling with laughter. "But everyone is at a disadvantage, not only just you. Oh my, when your uncle said he was sending you over, he did not say you had so much sass. You remind me so much of your mother."

I could see a tinge of sadness in both of their eyes.

"Well, nonetheless, let's get this game started." Aunt Charlotte clapped her hands.

I closed my eyes. Before I could begin counting, I sensed someone standing in front of me, feeling their breath on my cheek and the sweet aroma of perfume. Instinctively, my eyes flew open.

"You're not supposed to peep," said Aunt Charlotte, grinning. "Now, try again, and this time, keep them closed."

I shook my head at her, smiling. "One," I counted out loud when I closed my eyes a second time. I felt a whisper of movement to my right and strained to hear more. I couldn't tell who it was, but I thought someone had moved past me towards the window. "Two." I inserted the word *elephant* between counts, the way Aunt Charlotte taught me when I was younger. "Three."

This time I was certain I heard a giggle behind me, and I half-turned to work out who it was, but the instant I moved, it stopped.

"Four."

The faintest breeze brushed my arm – a door opening? Unfortunately, we hadn't determined which rooms the game should be confined to, and it was now too late to ask.

"Five." There was someone close to me still. "Six." A rustle in the vast entrance hallway. "Seven." Silence. All I could hear now was my heart thumping against my ribcage as though my life depended on winning the game. I rushed through the remaining numbers, "Eight ... nine ... ten. Coming, ready or not!"

I peered around the room. It seemed to peer back at me, giggling silently as though it knew something I didn't. On tiptoes, I walked towards the window. I couldn't be certain, but the long drapes looked slightly rumpled on the left and I was certain someone had passed me heading this way. Holding my breath, I reached out to touch the gold trimming along the edge of the material when the curtain suddenly puffed out and I felt a whoosh as someone flew past me.

"Maven!" I yelled. "No cheating."

Staying in the room, I searched behind the couches, behind the potted palms that reached the ceiling, inside my mother's dresser, where she kept her precious family silver. I even lay on the floor and scrutinized every inch of the room for a pair of feet. When I was convinced no one was there, I went out to the entrance hallway, where I'd heard rustling while I was counting.

My father kept a life-size statue of a giraffe under the staircase. I peeped behind this first. Then, I searched underneath the chaise-longue and the antique wooden tribal mask that was as tall as me. A sound behind me made me jump – it sounded like a mouse skittering beneath the floorboards for dropped crumbs. I crept stealthily back towards the giraffe as someone sneezed and a giant blue and white vase shook. It would have toppled over and smashed to pieces if I hadn't caught it. I peered inside and found Alek.

"How did you even fit in there?" I asked, laughing.

"Believe me; it wasn't easy."

I held the vase still while he clambered out. "You can help me look for Maven," I told him. I pressed a finger to my lips and pointed to the mannequin wearing a silk dress and pearls that my mother kept near the front door. "I think Maven went upstairs," I said loudly.

Catching on, Alek said, "I'll come with you."

He went to the bottom step and thumped loudly, so that Maven would think we were on our way upstairs while I waited for her to come out from behind the mannequin.

When she saw me waiting, her smile faded. "That's not fair," she said.

"You were cheating," I said. "*That's* not fair."

Maven folded her arms. "It's only a game, Sariyah."

"Well, now you can both help me find Kai and Aunt Charlotte."

"They went into the kitchen," said Maven.

"I hope they're not eating all the cake," said Alek.

Maven shook her head at him. "Do you ever think of anything other than your stomach?"

"Is there anything else to think about?" Alek laughed. As he was about to push the door into the kitchen, I heard a tinkle from the piano in the drawing-room.

"Wait," I said. I entered the drawing-room slowly. We rarely used this room and whenever I came in, I checked my hands to make sure they were clean. Now, with Alek and Maven behind me, hands clasped in front of them so that they didn't break anything, I crossed the room. I crept around the back of the piano, but no one was there. I crept around the front of it, and still no one. Back around and I dropped to the floor quickly to peer underneath it.

I rose, scratching my head. "I was certain I heard—"

Maven and Alek burst into laughter as Aunt Charlotte climbed off the piano stool where she'd been crouching so that I wouldn't spot her shoes. They told me she'd been sneaking around the piano while I'd been searching for her.

I hugged her tightly. "Only Kai to find now. Maven said he went into the kitchen."

"Oh, I don't think you'll find him there," said Aunt Charlotte. "If I know Kai, he'll be squeezed inside a cupboard, making himself look inconspicuous."

Together, we searched every cupboard we could find downstairs. The only room left was the kitchen and the ten minutes was almost up.

"I'll go first," I said, "and then we can split up inside."

I reached for the doorknob as the door burst open and Kai appeared carrying a cupcake on a china plate, a single candle fizzing on top. "Happy birthday!" he said, grinning.

"Kai!" I breathed in the aroma of the cupcake. "Strawberry?"

Kai nodded. "And strawberry frosting."

I examined the decoration around the top of the cake. The frosting was pink and shimmering and swirling like waves on the shore. "How did you know that was my favorite?"

"Aunt Charlotte told me," he said, glancing sideways at her and flashing her a smile. "I wanted it to be special. Now make a wish."

I took a deep breath and blew.

About the Author

Arricka writes to escape reality and dive into a world where the impossible is possible and adventure is guaranteed. Her love of writing began when she was in elementary school, but not in the way you might think. Arricka had a knack for being put in timeout because timeout meant the school librarian would make her pick a book to read quietly. (Don't tell anyone, but Arricka secretly loved timeouts.)

Today, she's still reading but in self-appointed timeouts from everyday business. Her favorite books include the: Thirst Series by Christopher Pike, The Vampire Diaries by L.J. Smith, The Vampire Academy by Richelle Mead, House of Night by PC and Kristen Cast, and 3 Dark Crowns by Kendare Black.

When Arricka isn't writing or reading, she can be found enjoying life with her two cats, Minnie and Midnight. The Clearwater, Florida native, now makes her home in Plant City, Florida. For more information about her or her books, visit the website: arrickawrites.com

Acknowledgements

There are quite a few people I would like to thank. Firstly, I want to thank my cousin Alexis. It is because of you that I was able to sit down and finally get this book completed. If we didn't have our talks about your book, I would have never gotten the courage to restart mine. Next, I would like to thank my best friend, Heather. I always run my ideas past you just to make sure I'm not crazy and you're always supportive of the good and the bad. Thank you for listening to my ideas and encouraging me to keep going even when it seemed like nothing was going my way.

I would also like to thank my friends Jae and Cate and Chris. I know yall were probably tired of me coming to work every day and or/ texting every day, going on and on about my book, but you listened and never made me feel like I was annoying. Thank you for reading my book and for giving me creative direction when needed. I would like to also thank my mother, Dana, for passing down her love of creative writing to me. Thanks to you, I fell in love with Nikki Giovani and Maya Angelou, which eventually led me to write my own poems and stories. It's great that we have something in common that is important to both of us.

To my parents Charlie and Karen, I am most grateful for you guys stimulating my love of reading and writing by taking trips to the library and to bookstores and for always allowing me to be self-indulged in my books instead of having to go outside and play. I may have left some people out, but rest assured, I am thankful to each person who has helped me on this journey. This book would just be random scribbles in an old notebook if not for you guys.

www.ingramcontent.com/pod-product-compliance
Lightning Source LLC
Chambersburg PA
CBHW021152110726
47900CB00002B/539